BROKEN CHAINS

KARINA KANTAS

Published by Dirty Streets Press

Paperback ©2021 ISBN: 978-1-912996-50-6

BROKEN CHAINS
© 2021 Karina Kantas

https:/urbanhype101.wordpress.com/

OTHER BOOKS BY KARINA KANTAS

The OUTLAW series
In Times of Violence
Huntress
Lawless Justice
Road Rage

Illusional Reality Duology
Illusional Reality
The Quest

YA supernatural thriller
Stone Cold

Collections
Heads & Tales
Undressed
A Flash of Horror

Dystopian sci-fi erotica
Toxic

Available in Audiobook
Illusional Reality book 1

Stone Cold

ACKNOWLEDGEMENTS

Huge thanks to my publisher and good friend at Dirty Streets Press.

Thank you for your support, your time, and for believing in me.

CONTENTS

BROKEN CHAINS

BROKEN CHAINS

PROLOGUE

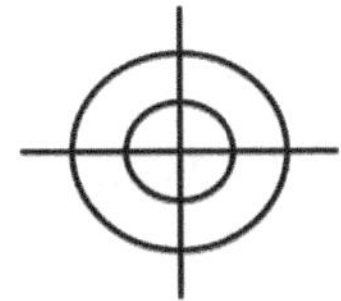

Liz had a mission, a secret one. Sitting in the coffee house, gazing out the window at an Italian architecture was not her idea of fun. But what she wanted was to capture the going-on of that building.

To further her masquerade, a glass of coke sat innocuously, still untouched, along with a small pad and pen on the table.

The elegance of the coffee house usually brought in the suits, but not being close to lunchtime, most of the executives were still in the offices. A casual glance from time to time around the room showed no one paid special attention to her. Now and again, someone would check her out, but there was no staring.

What caught Liz's interest was who was coming in and out of the building. She noted in a small pad the body language and attitude of each visitor, specific attention given to what they carried. Two men exited the building together but went off in separate directions. She jotted down her thoughts and justification. Liz wrote. 1. Leaving MI5 headquarters – one in casual dress, another wearing a suit. Why carry an umbrella when rain isn't forecasted. And the other appeared more like a lawyer, he wore a serious expression, the blue suit and tie and the brief case I wonder if he's trying too hard. Could it be a costume, a guise? They walked out the door together and then never glanced at one another and went separate ways 2. Serious expressions – Are they on a mission? Who are they, really – trouble? 3. Identification and destination? Subway, car?

What she needed were photographs. However, that would make it obvious, and she didn't want to seem like she was trying too hard. *I'm just casually sitting in a coffee shop glancing out a large window for the third time in a row. No harm in that is there?*

Her phone rang right on cue. She answered the call with one word, listening to the one-sided conversation. Keeping her sight on the building with a serious expression on her face, she nodded at appropriate times, making sure what she did say was relevant and easy to lip read. She closed the phone after a minute. Knowing the call would have already been traced.

Liz knew it was a dangerous game she was playing but was determined to see it through to the end. She had planned to return in two days and arrange another fake phone call. Liz gathered up her things and carelessly threw some change on the table. Two of the coins rolled off and landed on the floor, the sound of spinning metal seemed to echo through the room. Not wanting to waste time picking up the money, she turned away and exited the coffeehouse.

She had an inkling of what might happen, she'd been visualizing the scenario for weeks before she started putting MI5 to the test. She didn't know when, and what would occur, and it made the game more exciting. Nevertheless, the reality of the situation was very different. It was terrifying.

As soon as she saw the black Sedan, she knew they were coming for her. The huge car with shaded windows came around the corner, tyres screeching and drove onto the curb cutting off her path. Liz stepped back in fear. She knew she was in over her head.

***

Liz watched far too much TV, in particular crime thrillers such as *CSI, The Bill,* and her favourite, *Spooks.*

Spooks had become an obsession that had now gotten out of hand. Rather than recording the episodes, she would make sure she was always at home sitting beside the TV, notepad in hand, anticipating the next instalment. Printouts of her online research sat beside the computer monitor as did a job application to work for MI5, not that she was serious about applying. Again, just research. But she was curious about what qualifications someone would need for a position in the Secret Service.

However, it still wasn't enough. As soon as the DVDs came out, she was first in line to buy them. Liz had seen each episode a dozen times, noting the actor's approach in diverse situations, the resources MI5 had, and how the interrogations played out. The secrecy behind their double lives seemed exciting and the dangers they faced, thrilling. Liz wanted to know how realistic the program was, to see if Tom, the sexy main spy in *Spooks*, really existed. MI5's website denied any participation in underhand interrogations/investigations and yet the TV portrayed quite the opposite. And that's where the idea to write a thriller came from.

It started as a game, a test: proof, that *Spooks* portrayed the Secret Service convincingly. Would MI5 notice a person paying too much attention to their headquarters? Would they react, how would they react, and how anxious and curious would they become?

Would she base her main character on her actions so far? Would the protagonist be more intelligent? Was she an average joe, or was she going to be a spy? Maybe Russian?

As well as Liz pretending to be someone MI5 should be concerned about, thoughts about the book's plot and which way her main character would go played in her mind.

It was just research and she wondered if it would play out how she expected it to.

Now, sitting in the back of the black Sedan with two dark-suited men on either side, her imagination ran over time. It happened so fast she didn't have time to react or call out. One minute she was walking down the road, the next, they had snatched her bag and bundled her into the car.

How serious were they going to take her? Would they interrogate her? Was she in serious trouble? Maybe writing down, that she saw a female agent packing, was pushing it a little. Placing both hands on her lap, she squeezed them to stop them from shaking and inhaled the strong scent of leather and wondered how new the car was.

As she sat in silence, the car did a U-turn and entered

the gated Thames building. Liz wondered whether to play dumb or to start asking questions or own up and start pleading for them to let her go. On the other hand, she was about to step foot into MI5's headquarters and maybe even meet real-life agents. Wasn't that her intent? It was exciting in a scary way.

Liz tried to remain calm as the car drove underground and parked in a dark, secluded garage. The man sitting left to her grabbed her arm and pulled her out of the car and started dragging her towards a white aluminium door. It wasn't until the second man took out handcuffs from his jacket pocket that Liz reacted.

The driver had disappeared through another door leaving her alone with the two agents. First, she snatched her arm out of the grip the man had, then she backed away from them.

"You don't need to use them on me. I'll come quietly. You won't get any trouble from me. See I don't have any weapons on me." Liz opened her jacket, as she turned around to show them, she didn't have a gun concealed. The agents took their chance and tried to grab her. Catch her unaware, but life had shown her to always be ready and never turn your back on your enemies. *Are they, my enemy? Where did that come from? It's not like I'm a spy or working for Mafia.*

It would have been laughable, but the situation was now too frightening, and she didn't want to be there. And there was no way she was going to be handcuffed.

Although the agents defended themselves, they couldn't restrain her.

Using karate-chopping motions with her hands, she stopped

the men from grabbing hold of her. *Two against one is a little unfair. I don't want to hurt them, but there's no way I'm being restrained. I was coming in quietly. Why did they have to go this route? I'm going to defend myself with the tools I know.*

However, when she elbowed one agent in his gut, winding him, and then finished off with a smash to his nose, the men had had enough.

Bringing the flat of his hand down on the back of her neck, the unharmed man knocked her out.

When Liz regained consciousness, she found herself lying on a plain white plastic mattress in a white painted room. Synthetic odour awoke her senses. Sitting up, she rubbed her arms, but it wasn't from a chill. The room felt warm, even though there was nowhere for the heat to come in. She was about to call out when the cell door opened.

A woman in her late twenties came inside.

Liz thought the woman's smile was as fake as her tan.

"You've got yourself in a bit of a mess, haven't you?"

Liz stared back at the woman.

The grey pleated trouser suit she was wearing had to be designer and the high-heeled black leather shoes she wore added to the woman's already superior height. Not enjoying the feeling of being looked down upon, Liz stood up. Even though her neck still ached from the blow, she held her head up and faced the woman.

"Now, what is this all about?" the woman sang out and placed an arm around Liz's shoulder.

Liz shrugged it off.

The woman's sweet attitude changed.

"Let's go. People want to talk to you."

Liz followed the woman as they left the room. Three security guards were outside the door waiting to escort her. She'd learned her lesson and wasn't about to make the same mistake again.

Even though the walk was a short one, Liz made sure she had a good look around the place, taking in the metal and glass décor of the corridors and the numerous silver elevator doors. As they didn't come across another person, she assumed she was in a secure part of the building away from where the real work went on.

The woman led her to a plain grey door at the end of the corridor. As she opened the door, two suited men got up from their seats.

The room was small and square, sparse of décor and furniture. A grey coloured table sat in the centre of the room; the contents of her bag lay scattered on the top. A hand signalled for Liz to sit on the last chair. The woman nodded and then left the room.

A small monitor at the side of the room caught her attention. It was switched off, but not before Liz saw her white cell on the screen. They had been watching and recording her, no doubt they still were.

"Miss Finley, my name is Mr Smith, and this is Mr Jones."

Mr Jones nodded to Liz.

He wasn't quite like the Tom she'd imagined, but he had a pleasant appearance. Serious in a seductive way, he dressed to match. In a dark blue suit and polished black laced shoes, he looked smart but comfortable. Smith, on the other hand, was a rounded man, short with a balding head and scorn on his face.

Jones picked up Liz's note pad from the table and flicked through the pages.

"This makes interesting reading," he said, and then smiled.

Liz didn't think there was anything false about his smile. She felt warmth radiate from it.

"They're just notes," she answered.

"Argh, so she does speak." Jones laughed.

Smith took a beige folder from the table and started to read from it.

"Elizabeth Finley, known better as Liz. Age 24. Single, with no current boyfriend."

Liz swallowed hard.

"Mother deceased, father living somewhere in Greece."

"Shouldn't be too hard to track him down," Jones interrupted.

Smith nodded and then continued. "Income 12.000 per annually. 6.500 in savings at Barclay's bank. Oh, and you're allergic to peanuts."

He closed the file and threw it onto the table.

"Anything else you'd like to add, Miss Finley?" He folded his arms and glared at her.

"Call me Liz. No, I'm sure you know more about me than I do."

"Who are you working for?" Smith asked.

"You know who, it's in the file."

"Cut the crap, Liz." Smith slammed his fist down on the table.

She shifted in her chair. "I'm a singer in bars and clubs around town. The Golden Hawk in Bridge View Lane is my regular spot."

"Okay, let's start from the beginning," Smith said. "Why were you watching MI5 headquarters?"

Liz kept silent while she thought how to answer.

"God damn it," Smith yelled. "You've sat in Time Out Coffeehouse three times now, for exactly forty minutes. Watching the front of the building and taking notes. Why?"

The good cop, bad cop scenario was playing out like the TV programs, however, no one was going to shout 'cut, that's a wrap,' she worried.

"Research," she whispered.

"Research for what?" Jones asked.

"For a book, I'm writing. I'm an author, well trying to be."

Jones picked up the notebook again.

"You see a lot," he said. When he finished reading, he lifted his head and gazed at her.

"Too much," Smith added.

"Is it a crime to stare out a window?" Liz asked.

"Depends on what you're staring at," Smith answered.

"Look, this is stupid; do you really feel I'm a threat to national security? You're wasting your time." Liz leant forward and clasped her hands on the table.

"You seem to know a lot about what we do, who we are," Smith continued.

"Well, your names are certainly not Mr Jones and Mr Smith," Liz retorted.

Jones laughed.

"I watch a lot of TV, so yes, I have an idea about what goes on in here."

"Excuse my manners, Liz. Would you like a drink?" Jones asked.

"Yes. Thank you. Water, bottled with a sealed cap."

Jones grinned and shook his head before standing up and leaving the room.

"These are vivid descriptions, Liz. A couple of these people are Intelligence Officers, agents."

"I didn't know," Liz answered.

"But you had an idea, didn't you? I believe you knew who you were watching for, who you were keeping under surveillance."

"No, you've got it all wrong," Liz whined. "I'm no one you need to concern yourself with."

"Miss Finley, we take all potential threats seriously, for all we know you could be a terrorist."

Liz shook her head.

"Why were you watching MI5 headquarters?" he repeated.

"Research."

"Yes, research for your book. You said. But what's your book about?"

"Probably about a writer who sits opposite MI5 head-quarters, taking notes, researching her next novel, when she's kidnapped and interrogated."

Smith unbuttoned and took off his jacket. Which showed his overweighted belly. The buttons of his shirt being strained, ready to pop. Taking a handkerchief from his jacket pocket he wiped his sweaty brow.

Liz got the impression they were in for a long afternoon.

Taking his seat, he stared at Liz before asking. "Who were you talking to on the phone?"

"I'm sure you already know." Liz retorted.

"Stop playing this game, Liz. You're just digging your-self further in the hole you're already in."

"I haven't done anything wrong, jeez. I was sitting in the café thinking about my book, taking notes, and writing down ideas. You know, people watching. The phone call was from my neighbour, George Brown."

Jones came back into the room and handed Liz a small, chilled bottle of water.

"One water, chemical-free." He smirked. "Did you think we'd drug your drink?"

Liz shrugged her shoulders as she kept her gaze on Jones.

"You're too paranoid," Smith said.

"Am I?" Liz answered, staring at them both before unscrewing the cap.

Her throat parched and sore, she sipped the cool water gratefully. Her hand rubbed her sore neck and then rubbed the ache in her back.

Liz noticed Jones watching every movement.

"Would you like ice for your neck?" he asked.

"No. I'm okay."

"Why did you attack our two guards?" Smith asked.

"I freaked out when I saw the handcuffs. I was coming in quietly, so there was no need to restrain me."

"Security measures. Since the attacks, security has been heightened," Smith announced.

Liz nodded.

"Who trained you to fight?"

"No one trained me. I took self-defence classes."

Jones shook his head. "From what I saw, it was more than self-defence. Your movements flowed; you knew what you were doing. It was hardly an inexperienced show. So, shall we try again? Where did you learn martial arts?"

"Jeez, I work in a bar, okay? You can't imagine the jerks we get in there. The drunks think I'm free property."

"I'm assuming they have security," Smith asked.

"I can take care of myself."

"Yes, we saw that," Jones said.

The two men whispered to one another and then stood up. Jones leaned in towards Liz.

"Take this time to sort your story out. It's not looking good for you, Liz. You're going to have to do a better job at convincing me of your innocence."

"I am innocent," she yelled as Smith and Jones left Liz alone in the room.

She stared at the bare walls, her mind replayed scenes from *Spooks*, where members of the public were warned off and some even disappeared when they were thought as being high risk or became too interested in an agent. Liz shivered. But then again it was just TV. The MI5 website stated they worked within the law. *Only it wouldn't be too difficult to make me disappear, she mused. No one would worry about me.* She sighed as the realization of how alone she was, caused her to want to evaluate her life. *We only have one life to live and I'm not going anywhere on the path I'm on. I need adventure, thrills. I'm not too sure I'm going to find it by writing my book.*

Surely, they aren't thinking about charging me. Do they honestly feel I'm a threat to national security? Liz cursed herself. What did she expect? She'd done everything to seem as though she could be a problem. However, it was all a game, wasn't it? All part of the research. She saw herself back in the Time Out Coffee house and imagined what was going on inside the building. *I'm over my head! What have I done? Are they going to arrest me? How long will I be kept here? There's no one to help me, no friends I can call. No fucking evidence that this was a test as part of my research. I'm screwed.* Liz started biting her nails as she thought about the implications of her actions. *I wish I never thought about writing this thriller. I wish I used my head and stopped. The research I found online and the notes I took from the TV series Spooks, would have been enough. But fuck I've screwed up.*

Liz realised that if she wanted to leave MI5 headquarters, she needed to be honest. Tired, with her neck still in pain, she folded her arms on the table and rested her head, closing her eyes shutting off the entire world

The nap was a welcome one, but as they had removed her watch, she had no idea how much time had passed. Feeling restless, she stood up and stretched. The contents of her bag still littered the table. Picking up her notepad, she read what she had written.

It read to her as research, but then again it also read as though she was keeping surveillance. Especially how detailed the notes were and her thoughts about each person who left the building

Well, the woman seemed like an agent, I could see the outline of her gun holster on the outside of her jacket and who would exit the Thames building with a bag of nappies under their arm? Yes, she could have bought them for someone or herself, but the gun, showing she was packing, made it obvious to me she was an agent, maybe even undercover. Liz mused. The people' descriptions were well-detailed, perhaps too detailed, and she had yet to give them any solid evidence she wasn't an agent herself.

More time passed before the door opened again.

Jones came into the room alone, and after placing the

beige folder on the table, he sat down. Liz took the seat opposite him.

"Are you hungry?" he asked.

"No, I just want to go home. This is all wrong. I'm not what you think I am."

"And what do I think you are?"

"A spy, a terrorist maybe. I can understand why it may seem like that, but I'm just a singer in a band. Nothing more."

"I want to believe you, Liz," Jones said, grasping her hands and squeezing them.

Surprised by his forwardness she couldn't deny the reassuring gesture was what she needed.

"But you haven't told me anything to think otherwise," he continued. "It's not just your actions which worry me. It's your attitude. You haven't shown any emotions. It's as though you've been trained to handle interrogations. Any average Joe would have broken down in tears by now, but you're a hard nut to crack, Liz. It's as though you're putting on an act, a show. I want to see the real you."

He stroked her hand and smiled.

"What you see is what you get," Liz said, removing her hand. "It takes a lot to make me cry. I guess I've built a wall, and it's hard for me to let people in, and trust me, Jones. I have never been interrogated before and it's never going to happen again. Let me go and you'll never see me anywhere near this street again. I promise.

Jones leaned back into his chair and studied her.

"We checked. The call was from a George Brown. What I want to know is why you used the expression…" Jones took out a folded piece of paper from his jacket pocket and read aloud. "'Yes, more than likely. I will follow and check-in with you in an hour. No, not much activity.'"

He finished reading and pushed the paper across to Liz. She didn't need to read the conversation; she knew what she'd said.

"It was a test. All of it was a test."

"What do you mean?" Jones asked.

"I wanted to see if I could get a reaction from MI5 if I appeared and acted as a potential threat. I'm not working for anyone.

"So, it was all an act, a test for us?"

"Yes, but I seriously didn't think for one second it would work. You see, I'm a fan of the TV series *Spooks*. I'm sure you know it?"

Jones shook his head.

"Well, I've always wondered how realistic the show was. I wanted to see for myself. I wish I hadn't now. I saw too much. I noticed things about the people leaving MI5, their mannerisms my thoughts about where they were going next. I'm a storyteller so I made up their story on what their assignment was. I assume the average Joe wouldn't have noticed anything strange. I guess it's a cursed gift. You have to realise it was just research."

"For your book?" Jones finished.

Liz nodded.

"And you learned how to attract and entice MI5 from the TV program?"

"And common sense," Liz added.

"If you'd used common sense, you wouldn't be in this mess," Jones replied.

For the first time since the interrogation started, Liz laughed.

Jones cracked a smile and then took the folder from the table and sat reading for a few moments before speaking again.

"Okay, Liz, I believe you. Let's see if I can get you home without any charges. I've never watched *Spooks*, but I've heard about it and if it's going to cause members of the public to waste our time and resources, then maybe it should be cancelled."

Liz swallowed hard; the word cancelled made her uneasy.

"Out of interest, what attracts you to the program?"

"I guess it's the danger. The seriousness, way the agents work. They can just walk away and live a double life, without thinking twice. It's exciting. They get to do a job and serve their country at the same time. Jones, I'm sorry for wasting your time. I never thought it would play out like this. I didn't realize how much trouble I'd be causing."

"Tell me, Liz, what's an educated woman like you doing working as a singer in bars?"

"It's all I'm good at, and I enjoy it," she answered defensively.

"I wouldn't say it's your only skill. You've shown yourself to be very receptive, intelligent, and you have an excellent flair for observation." Jones paused. "Okay, let me talk to my supervisor and see if we can get you home. Are you sure you wouldn't like a coffee or something?"

"No. Thank you. I just want to go home and pretend this never happened."

Jones smirked, resting his hand on her shoulder; he then got up and left the room, closing the door behind her.

The warmth of his touch lingered, as did the scent from his cologne which smelt of woodland and pinecones.

The beige folder lay open on the table, and although Liz was curious, she knew they'd be watching her and snooping through personal files, even if it was hers, wouldn't get her home for tea. Liz breathed a huge sigh. She had the research she wanted, but at what cost? It was certain they'd be keeping tabs on her. She'd never stolen from a shop before, never missed paying a parking ticket, never broken the law in her life, and now she was probably MI5's blacklist, and all for the sake of her art. Jeez, the publishers would have to take her seriously now.

They allowed Liz to leave Thames building half an hour later after Smith had scrutinised her background and was satisfied Liz wasn't a potential threat. She never thanked Jones.

***

Back home, life had changed for Liz. She remembered what Jones had said to her. Was she intuitive, did she have a good eye? The realisation of just how alone she was, caused her to evaluate her life. She had no close friends, no boyfriend, no one she could confide in or who would miss her if she vanished. She didn't feel comfortable in her life, and she soon lost her passion for singing, going through the motions without thought. She felt bored and came to the same conclusion every time she became restless. She needed excitement and wanted to take a few risks in her life. She needed thrills. The adrenaline rush. The book was forgotten now. Liz decided she wanted to live the fiction rather than write it

***

A year had passed fast for Liz. She continued to sing now and again, but her days were filled with work and her nights studying. There was no room for boredom. She knew she'd made the right decision in a career change, proving to her university tutors and government supervisors they were right to take a chance on her.

Liz was sitting in her living room revising for a test when the doorbell rang.

Slipping the security chain across the lock, she opened the door and was surprised to see Jones on the opposite side. Casually dressed, his hair appeared longer. Her stomach fluttered as he smiled at her.

"Hi, Liz, remember me?" He grinned.

She shut the door, removed the chain, and then opened the door wide.

"Hi, umm come in." Liz watched as Jones entered the living room.

Her pulse throbbed like the ticking of a clock. The attraction she had for him seemed to quadruple since the last time they met. She hoped he wouldn't hear the sudden pounding of her heart.

"I'm not disturbing you, am I?" he asked.

"No. It's nice to see you again." She blushed. "Please, take a seat. Would you like a drink?"

"No, thanks."

"Are you on duty?"

"I'm always on the clock." He laughed.

"What I meant was, is this an official call? I'm wondering what I've done this time. I swear to you I haven't even walked past the Thames building."

"I know." Jones smiled. "You've been keeping busy."

"Nothing gets past you. Does it, Mr Jones?"

"Call me Alex."

"Is that your real name? Sorry, you don't have to answer that."

"Yes, Alex is my real name." He smiled.

"Nice to meet you, Alex," Liz said, holding her hand out.

The two shook hands. His large hand engulfing hers. She was the first to let go.

"I'm here unofficially on official business," he said.

"Well, that makes sense." Liz laughed, as she sat down on the sofa beside him. Crossing her legs, she placed both hands on her knees and then turned towards him.

"So, what can I do for you?" she asked.

"We would like to offer you a job."

"What! Working at MI5?"

Alex nodded.

"In what capacity?"

"You'll start as an administrative assistant, a paper pusher."

"Is that a code name for something else?" Liz smiled at her joke.

Alex laughed. "No, it means you'll be drafting documents, organising meetings and so forth. You'll learn the ropes, and if you work hard and prove yourself, which I know you will, you'll move up the ranks."

"You have a lot of faith."

"I knew when I met you that you had a special talent. I was hoping you might think about a career change."

"I haven't even graduated yet. What if I don't pass?"

"That's unlikely. You're at the top of your class. Your

superiors give you nothing but praise. I can see how much your confidence has grown. You've shown yourself to have a great personality, integrity, reliability, discretion, and excellent organisation skills. You've passed every exam and have proven yourself an asset to any government department."

"You have been keeping a watch on me. So, I'm not the same nutcase you interrogated then?"

"No, even then your special qualities were noticed." He grinned and again her stomach fluttered. "I knew you weren't a danger to national security but as the current level of threat was severe, we had to make sure. As soon as I heard you'd started your training, I've been keeping an eye on your progress. I'm hoping it was our meeting and not the TV program *Spooks* which founded your decision."

"Both." Liz smiled.

"You don't still watch it, do you?"

"God, no! I'm surprised you guys didn't cancel the show."

"Nah, it's good entertainment."

"I feel stupid for taking the program so seriously. I thought that was how MI5 worked."

"If we went around assassinating members of the public, we would have been shut down years ago."

"I know. Like you say, *Spooks* is just entertainment."

"Working for MI5 is a lot more fun. Hell, more exciting than the program."

"I believe you, Alex."

"Okay," He cleared his throat. "The formalities. You've already signed Section One of the Official Secrets Act, but we have our own you'll need to sign; oaths that will need to be taken. Although you won't be in the role of an investigating officer, you will need to be trained. There's always the chance you might be picked up. You'll have a lot of national security secrets at your fingertips and people will do anything for that information. You'll need to be prepared."

"I understand," Liz answered.

"I'm sure I don't have to remind you not to tell anyone you're a member of the Secret Service. The work you will be doing is sensitive and discretion is vital. As you've already gone through the vetting process you won't have to wait the usual six months while checks are made."

"No, I've already completed all the questionnaires and had a meeting with the DV officer before I started working for the Home Office."

Alex nodded, then continued. "There'll be formal training both internal and external. Plus, there will be management development programs and language training facilities."

Liz waited until he'd finished speaking before asking, "Is it okay if you tell me what you do?"

"I'm one of the heads from the Intelligence Department. We work alongside MI6, assessing potential threats and monitoring suspected terrorist networks. I'm a spy and agent, but we prefer to use the name Intelligence Officers."

"Will I be working in your department?" Liz asked as she shuffled in her chair.

"Not at first." Liz frowned. "Don't worry we'll see a lot of each other. MI5 encourages internal relationships." Alex's face started to turn pink. "What I meant was they prefer interdepartmental relationships."

Liz knew she was blushing. Even so, she wouldn't turn away from his face; his soft lips, sexy smile and seductive eyes were mesmerizing.

"Umm…you'll have to move from here," he continued. "You'll be given one of our apartments. They get swept for bugs often. They're reserved for agents, but as you will be trained to assist me, I thought it prudent for you to have an established cover. What puts you ahead, is you have no close relatives or friends – sorry."

"No, it's alright."

"It just means it's easier for your cover, is what I meant."

Reaching out she touched his knee. "It's okay, Alex, I get it." She removed her hand. "So, when do I start packing?"

"Let's wait until your graduation before relocating you. I'd rather you weren't distracted. I'd like you to come down to headquarters, get a feel for the place. I'll introduce you to a few people so your first day won't be so daunting. You've been working down at the Home Office for a while now. How's it going?"

"Interesting, I'm learning a lot."

"But you need excitement." Alex smiled. "I can see it in you. Be patient, Liz. It will happen for you."

He stood up to leave. "I'll be in touch soon."

Liz showed him to the front door.

"Thank you, Alex. Thank you for having confidence in me."

He smiled. "I'm looking forward to us working together. Study hard and ace that exam. Keep this discussion between the two of us, okay?"

"Don't worry, you can trust me," Liz replied.

CHAPTER ONE

The Final Test

She'd almost finished her training in physical and weapon combat and was about to start her advanced training. Alex had told her that if she passed, she would be a qualified Investigating Officer. Liz now knew the way MI5 worked and who and what was handled in each department. She was a regular face around the office and was liked and respected by her colleagues.

Alex was keeping a watchful eye on her and kept pushing until he thought she was ready for her first assignment. Although it was labelled as risk-free and categorised low in importance, Liz didn't want to fail Alex and herself. She knew he had put himself on the line for her and if it didn't run smoothly, he would be the one facing flack not her.

Her assignment was easy enough. She was to meet a contact in a local pub and receive a telephone number that she had to memorize. Part of her training was storing numbers, information and trying to decipher codes.

Liz was about to leave her apartment and meet the contact when her private mobile rang. Her number wasn't listed, and the line was untraceable, so she knew the call was from headquarters.

"Hello," she answered.

"Just wanted to wish you good luck, not that you'd need it," Alex said. Liz could tell he was grinning on the other line. "Listen, I'm going to be doing surveillance on this, just for training purposes," he added. "I'll be in the blue Astra just left of the pub. Meet me there when you're done."

"I'm not wired," she said.

"Are you going to wear the jean jacket as we agreed?" he asked.

"Yes."

"Then, you're wired," he replied.

"Ah, okay. I'll see you soon," she said, and then closed the phone and put it inside her shoulder bag. Liz stared in the hallway mirror one last time and smoothed down the sides of her long bobbed, brunette hair. Wearing blue jeans and a casual pink top, she stared at the blue jacket that hung on the hook beside the door. It wasn't until she was wearing the jacket that she noticed the badge pinned on the lapel.

"Good choice," she said aloud and stroked the Iron Maiden Badge. She imagined Alex listening with a grin on his face.

The air outside was bitter, so she fastened the last three buttons on her jacket then walked down the white, marble steps and turned left towards the bus stop. There were already three people waiting for the bus into town. Liz gave them the once over and smiled at an elderly lady.

"Looks like rain," the woman said.

"Damn, I knew there was something I forgot," Liz replied.

Cheery banter followed and then the bus arrived.

Alex was sitting inside the Astra making sure sound wasn't distorted. He was already watching live feedback from inside the pub, thanks to the landlord's secret security camera.

He saw the contact enter the pub and walk over to the bar. The man turned his head towards the door too many times for Alex's liking. Change dropped from the guy's hand as he tried to pay for his pint. Alex didn't like the way the guy was acting. Something was up. For a moment he thought about ringing Liz and aborting the mission, but then he decided he'd watch and see if anything else unusual occurred. He was eager to see her in action and watch how she'd handle things, but there was no way he would allow her to walk into danger. There wasn't enough evidence to go on just his gut instinct, which would, as usual, turn out to be right. Pulling out his mobile phone, he laid it on his knee, ready just in case.

Liz took out her mobile and answered the call.

"Sure, I'll be there in five. Order me a pint." She smiled and then closed the phone.

It wasn't part of the script, but she wanted it to appear she was meeting a friend, should someone be following her or listening. Her training taught her to be cautious and suspicious of everyone.

Alex wondered who she was talking to and then putting himself in the same situation, smiled when he realised what she did.

"Good girl," he said.

By the time Liz entered the pub, the contact was sitting by a table in the corner of the bar almost hiding from view, she thought. The place was large, but dingy with thread-bare red and gold carpet lining the floor and scratched dark wooden furniture. It had been a while since the place had been decorated, she mused.

Walking over to the bar she ordered a diet coke and then scanned the rest of the pub. For a Friday after-noon, the bar was quiet as usual. A couple of suited businessmen were sitting by a table engrossed by the Daily Telegraph newspaper. A couple sat by the bar eat-ing chips from a basket. Her nose caught the smell of grease and vinegar. Turning her head, she saw a young guy dressed in casual jeans and a jumper, playing on the fruit machine. Another two guys were propping up the bar and having a quiet conversation. Liz took a seat and glanced in the contact's direction. The man shook his head. It was just a small shake but enough to be noticed if someone else had been watching, and enough for her to conclude that something was up. She remained at the bar and sipped her drink while checking her watch every minute, feigning impatience. She gave up waiting and pulled her phone out.

"Hey. Where are you? I've been waiting ten minutes," she said, loud enough to be heard by those close by. "Oh, I see. Okay. No – don't worry. I'll catch up with you later. Sounds like fun but I can't make it, something's come up. You know how it is. No, don't change your plans. I'll sort something out. Okay. Yeah, see you soon. Bye."

Liz hoped Alex would get the message.

Draining her glass, she then called the barman over.

"Where's the ladies' room?" she asked.

He pointed to the door at the end of the bar opposite

where the contact was sitting. She walked towards the contact and gave a huge smile.

"John, wow! What are you doing back here? It's been ages." She walked up to the man and hugged him like a long-lost friend. With luck, the man understood what she was doing and played along.

"Hi, Chris. You look great. How's the kids?"

"Doing good, thanks. So how long have you been in town? Why didn't you call?"

"I only got back a couple of days ago," he answered, and stopped talking. She felt his nerves and knew she needed to get away from him as soon as she could before he gave the game away. Even if it meant failing her mission.

Liz reached over and touched his arm. "I'm sorry I can't stay and chat. I've got to run, but we'll catch up soon, yeah?"

"You want my number?" the man asked hopeful, his eye shone with hope.

She wanted to kick the guy in the kneecap for being so blatantly obvious.

"Nah, I've still got it." She smiled. Then leaning towards his cheek, she whispered. "Leave it in the men's toilet, third cubicle." Her lips barely touched his cheek before she pulled away with a smile and then walked off towards the ladies. She did her business, then waved at her friend before leaving the pub.

Liz noticed Alex sitting in the car, but instead of getting in like she was supposed to, she crossed the road and walked in the opposite direction. She did some window shopping and had some lunch before returning to her apartment. In that time, she never let her guard drop; checking window reflections of the people around her; searching for familiar faces from the pub or ones that kept appearing while she did her lengthily detour around the busy town.

***

Alex watched Liz walk away and then waited ten minutes before using the back door of the pub and slipping into the gents, unnoticed. He located the number which had been scribbled on tissue paper and stuffed it behind the water pipes. Pulling out a lighter, he burned the evidence then exited unnoticed from the bar.

***

Neither spoke to one another until work the following morning, where Liz was summoned to head office to report on what happened.

"We've listened to the tapes and watched the recording. What gave you the impression there was a problem?" the director asked.

"It was where he was positioned, sir. Of all the places he could have sat in the bar he picked a corner table hidden from view. It was supposed to be a friendly meeting, not a covert operation. The subject then indicated for me not to approach."

"So, why didn't you abort?" he asked.

"I'd just been given my first assignment. I wasn't about to let my team down. I knew I could get the information if I approached it in the right way."

"Yes, that was good thinking. Well, you'll be happy to know that Officer Alex retrieved the information we needed. So, all in all, a good job done." He shuffled his papers, indicating that the meeting was over.

"Sir, if I may speak?"

He nodded to her.

"I didn't get the impression that I was being watched, and I covered my tracks carefully, but I think the contact was."

"Yes, you may be right, Liz. The man in question has gone missing. We haven't been able to reach him."

Liz digested the information. It could only mean one thing.

"So, what went wrong? This was supposed to be a low-risk assignment. Sorry, sir," she added, realising she shouldn't have spoken out.

"It was categorised as low risk for the officer, not the contact. That will be all, Miss Finley."

Liz left the office, not sure how she should be feeling. Should she feel elated that she'd pulled off her first assignment or disturbed and upset that a man she'd just met might have been killed?

Back in the office, Alex opened and walked through the side door and stood in front of the director's desk.

"Well, the woman can certainly use her head, and she's quick on her feet, but I'm not sure she's strong enough to cope with fieldwork," the director said, leaning back in his chair.

"Give her a break, Jack," Alex answered. "It was supposed to be a simple task. Who knew it was going to turn out like that? It's her first taste of the job, now she's been christened I think you'll see just how strong Liz can be.

"Hmm… So, you think it's time to put her out in the field?"

Alex nodded.

"Do you think she's up to it?" the director asked.

"I think she'll surprise you," Alex said, the smile tightening around his mouth.

"Okay, set it up. I suppose it best to know whether she's up for the job, rather than waste taxpayers' money to train someone who's not competent."

***

Liz got the call late Wednesday morning. She walked into the conference room and was surprised to see it full. The director was seated at the head of the table; he stood up as she walked in.

"Please take a seat, Miss Finely."

She glanced at Alex before sitting on the last chair. His face was unreadable.

Hart, Chief of Intelligence, stood up and pressed a button on the remote he was holding. The back screen flashed up and the face of a Japanese man appeared.

"Okay, this is the last photo we have of Yazumi. He went underground two years ago and has just resurfaced. We've been after this guy for a while now. He's connected to the Haki terrorist group. We know that he has in his possession a disk, which contains data on future terrorist campaigns which the Haki group intends to implement. I can't stress to you how important it is that we get hold of this man and, if possible, bring Yazumi in for questioning."

Hart sat down and then Alex stood up. "There's a team standing by ready to extract Yazumi. Liz, I want you on this. You're to go undercover as Teresa Blake, a beautician at the salon where Yazumi frequents. That's where we're going to take him down. He doesn't trust anyone with the disk and so carries it with him everywhere. Find the disk and bring it here. The rest of the team will be standing by to bring him in. Everything you need to know is in the file. Read up and be ready to leave in one hour."

"Any questions?" Director Hart asked.

Papers were shuffled, quiet murmuring began, and then the room started to empty.

Liz wanted to speak to Alex. She touched his arm and then stood back and waited until they were alone.

"Can this source of intel be trusted?" she asked.

"What do you mean?"

"Well, it just seems that if this guy is walking around with such an important disk in his pocket that he's gonna have armed security wherever he goes."

"And?" Alex interrupted.

"So why would he risk the disk and his life for a visit to a salon when he could easily get a manicure, spa or whatever, done at home."

He raised his eyebrows before shrugging. "Maybe he likes being pampered in public. Look, I don't know if we can trust the source, but this is the first opportunity we've had to catch this guy, and we can't let him walk."

"It just seems odd that he should start showing his face now. It's like he's not afraid anymore."

"Just read up on the intel and then get to wardrobe, they're waiting for you. I'll brief you on tactics before you leave." Alex walked away before she could ask any more questions.

***

Dressed in a pink smock with a white apron, Liz tied her head up in a bun while listening to the rest of the team talking strategy. Clipping on the salon's logo pin on the top left side of her smock, she tested the transmitter.

"Testing one-two."

The man sitting by the computer held the earphones close to his ears and then signalled with his thumb.

"How are you feeling?" Alex asked as he adjusted the pin.

His sudden appearance. made her jump. She was on edge, but it wasn't from fear.

"Fine," she answered.

"Just be alert and expect the unexpected. I know you'll do fine."

His hands rested on her shoulders; she saw the concern etched on his face.

"Remember what you've been taught. You're good at evaluating people and situations, so use your head. If it doesn't feel right, get out."

***

Everything was going to plan. Liz was inside busying herself with customers when Yazumi walked in.

The way he holds himself, not smiling at anyone, makes it obvious he's not a man to be messed with. Out of the corner of her eye, she watched the receptionist try to take his coat. Yazumi laid it over his left arm and scowled at her before being greeted by the head beautician.

Liz went into the stock room to replace an empty bottle of shampoo. Making sure no one was around; she spoke into the pin.

"Subject has entered the building. He's booked in for aromatherapy treatment, that's when I'm going to make my move."

Another beautician entered the room. "Teri when you're done can you bring Mr Yazumi a fruit smoothie?"

"Sure, where is he?"

"He's in the tranquil room. Chop chop. Don't want to keep this customer waiting. Trust me."

Liz smiled and then grabbed a shampoo bottle and left the room.

***

Yazumi was lying down asleep. As Liz walked inside, holding a glass of juice in her hand.

Yazumi was wearing a black eye mask. His hands loosely clasped on his chest. Large black earphones covered his ears. The strong incense that was burning was enough to put anyone to sleep, she thought. Knowing he couldn't see or hear her; she went over to his jacket that was now hanging folded over a chair behind the leather therapy couch. The pocket was right in front of her.

"This is too easy. Something feels off." Ignoring her doubts she reached into the inside pocket, and she felt the disk, but just as she was about to take it out, she sensed a presence behind her. It took but a moment to decide not to fight and instead try and talk herself out of the situation.

She turned to see Yazumi standing up, staring at her, very alert.

"What do you think you're doing?" he asked with an accent that sounded Japanese, but Liz also heard the

English twang that would have come from someone who had lived in the UK for a long time.

"Sorry, sir, your jacket was on the floor. I was putting it back on the chair for you." She knew she wasn't fooling anyone.

Before she had time to act, Yazumi grabbed her arm and twisted behind her back.

"Who are you?" he growled.

A side door opened before she had time to utter another word. Two men came running in and tried to grab her. Liz fought them off. Busting one man's nose with the flat of her hand, and then using karate she swept her left foot out and floored the other man. As she spun around to face Yazumi, an HK PC7 stopped her in her tracks. The gun was pointed at her head.

"Turn around slowly," Yazumi said.

***

Liz woke and found herself bound to a wooden chair in a small room, which smelled as though it could have been a disused barn. The small bulb that swung from the breeze gave off enough light for her to see just one exit. *What the hell happened? Where's my backup and where the hell am I?* The gag tied across her mouth, allowed her to breathe with ease, but not to call out, not that she had any intention of attracting her abductor's attention. She struggled with the binds that held her feet and hands, but as they were plastic cuffs that tightened the more, she struggled, she soon gave up. They were professionals, she concluded, and she knew there was a high possibility that she was being held by the Haki. She was still wearing her pink uniform, but when she searched for the pin, it was missing. Just the action of bending her head made her vision spin from the hit she took from Yazumi's gun. The intense pain made her want to cry out. Instead, she squeezed her eyes wanting to block the pain. She hoped that MI5 had managed to track her location before the transmitter had been destroyed.

The interrogation started when three masked men entered the room. All three were dressed in identical black combat trousers, a black polo-neck jumper, and polished black combat boots. Each carried a weapon; each wore a white-faced mask. They surrounded her before one of them removed the gag and then the men separated. One stood by the door; his arms folded. The tallest of the men stood to the right, and the last man was in front of her.

Liz had to make a quick decision, one that could save or wreck her chances of survival. Should she play the tough agent and not answer any of their questions, be strong and unaffected by their tactics or play the innocent helpless woman, who has no idea why they've taken her? However, these guys gave her the impression that they wouldn't stand for any attitude.

"Why am I here? What do you want?" she cried.

"Listen carefully," the man in front of her said. Again, she noticed a weak Japanese accent, mixed with a British. "We can do this the hard way or the easy way. Just answer our questions and you'll leave here in one piece. Be stupid, and you're in for a lot of hurt. Understand?"

She nodded. "Please don't hurt me. Please, I don't know why I'm here."

The man ignored her.

"What's your name," he barked.

"Sue Clayton," she answered.

"Who do you work for, Miss Clayton."

"I'm a beautician at Top 2 Toe. I'm sorry I touched Mr Yazumi's jacket. I didn't think I was doing anything wrong."

The man stepped forward, grabbed a chunk of her hair, and pulled her head back.

"Don't play games with me," he yelled. "Who do you work for?"

"I told you," She shouted. "I'm a beautician at Top 2 Toe. Please, what's this about?"

The man then pulled out a blindfold from his trouser pocket and tied it around her head.

"What have I done wrong? I'm sorry. Please don't hurt me?" she begged.

Liz didn't know what was going to happen next, but she knew she had to try to stick to her cover no matter what happened.

Hands started ripping off her clothes. She felt them on her skin, touching her legs. There were sniggers. The men were enjoying their work. Were they going to sexually assault her? She never felt so helpless in her life. Knowing she was sitting bound and unable to defend herself, knowing they were watching her, staring at her half-naked body, staring at her most private parts. She felt ashamed. Why couldn't she be fat and have a figure that would repulse them rather than a curvy, voluptuous body that was going to excite them? She couldn't see them. She couldn't hear them, but she knew they were there.

The voice was close; she felt his breath on her ear.

"I'm going to ask you again. What is your name?"

"Please believe me," she whimpered. "Sue Clayton."

The first zap occurred on her left arm. The electric shock burned through her skin and travelled down her arm to the tips of her fingers. Her body jolted from the touch, and she cried out.

"Please stop. Why are you doing this?"

"Who sent you to steal the disk from Yazumi? Who are you working for?" A different voice asked one that carried a distinctive Japanese accent, not like her first interrogator.

"What disk. I don't know what you're talking about."

Another shock, this time to her right leg. The leg jerked upwards, and the pain carried up into her gut. Her body was still shaking after they removed the Taser. Even though she couldn't move much, the cuffs on her wrists cut into her skin.

Liz felt sick. Her skin itched and tingled with pain, while her head throbbed. How long did she have until they zapped her again? Which part of the body were they going to strike next? Sweat dripped down her face and formed a puddle on her neck.

"We can make this all go away. You can walk out of here if you tell us who you're working for." The first interrogator spoke.

"Why are you doing this? I don't understand?" She cried, and they were real tears. She was scared. *I don't know how much longer I can keep up this act. I don't know how much more of this I can take.*

The next electric hit got her in the right side of her ribs. The intensity of the current was such that her body jumped; the chair fell back taking her with it. Her head slammed onto the concrete floor causing her head to ache and become lightheaded.

"Why are you making this hard?" he whispered. "We know who you're working for. So, you might as well tell us. Why keep lying? It's gonna get worse for you."

If they already knew, what would be the harm in telling them? she thought. They would keep torturing her until they got what they wanted. Maybe if she played along with them, they'd go easier on her.

The electric current started from her left foot and travelled up her leg. She couldn't breathe, her chest tightened, her whole body was wracked in pain.

"Okay, no more," she screamed, her breathing coming out in pants. "I'll tell you what you want to know."

She sensed the men stepping away from her. But she didn't have the energy to lift her head.

"We want the names of the other agents you work with." The Japanese man said.

So that's what they're after. It would be easy enough to give them the names but what good would it do? I only know them by their alias. Alex is the only identity I know, and even then, it's just his first name. and there was no way I'm going to speak it, no matter what they do to me.

"Please," she cried. "I don't know what you're talking about."

Another hit, this time to the chest. It was enough for Liz to pass out, but not before she felt a hand take her wrist and hold it in a way a doctor would be reading a pulse.

She wasn't sure how long she'd been out. But when she came to, she was alone; still in her underwear, but no longer bound to the chair. The smell of sweat and electricity filled the room. Liz was too weak to try to lift her head or attempt to get off the chair. Her muscles ached, her mouth dry and her lips were sore. The red burn mark on her left foot laughed at her stupidity. All she had to do was tell them the names she knew. It wasn't her fault if they were false identities. There was no need to have gone through the suffering. They weren't her friends. Why should she suffer to protect them? What had they ever done for her?

After the guilt came the fear: What were they going to do to her next? How long would it continue until she told them everything? Then the anger: Where was her back up? Why hadn't someone rescued her? Did they think she was expendable, not worth the effort? Well, she'd show them. If they didn't give a shit about her, why should she go through the agony of torture for them?

She heard the door open and saw three sets of feet coming towards her. A hand grabbed her hair and pulled her head back.

"How we doing there? Still with us. We don't want to lose you just yet."

It then occurred to her that no matter what they did or what she said, they were going to kill her. From somewhere she found a hidden strength. If she was going to go, she was going down fighting.

Taking a deep breath, she opened her eyes wide and turned her head to see her abductor. Her vision blurred from the strain, but she glared at him and said, "Let me go you piece of shit, or you'll be sorry."

The man lashed out with such force it knocked her off the chair onto the dusty floor. Her heart raced, her head pulsated, and she squeezed her eyes shut taking her mind and pain to another place.

The sound of feet running over toward her woke up

her senses again. She was picked off the floor and sat back in the chair. Her arms were bound to the back of it with thick rope. One of the men slapped her, causing her to be alert again. Her hair was pulled back, and she screamed as one of the men held her head in a tight grip while the other covered her mouth with cling film. Panic at not being able to breathe, knowing she was suffocating, forced her pulse rate to rise and her whole body to fight in defence. She struggled in their grips. The third man grabbed her chin and held it while he started pouring water onto the plastic gag. She closed her eyes and screamed as the water splashed over her face, and up her nose, choking, drowning her. The interrogation technique lasted a few moments, but to Liz, it was a lifetime. When they removed the cling film and allowed air to flow back into her mouth and lungs, the first man stood over her and screamed into her face.

"Your name?"

"Teresa Blake," she cried back.

The words worked like magic. Their grip was released, and her head gently laid on the chest of a man standing behind her. She opened her eyes to see the men removing their masks. Liz knew there was no way she was going to be leaving the room. She'd seen their faces. They weren't going to let her live. *Something has changed. They're being gentle and I don't feel the tense atmosphere anymore. What trick are they playing now? What do they want!* A hand lifted her head and then wiped a cloth over her wet face. Another man knelt by the chair and cut her binds. The other two of them tried to lift her off the chair, but her legs gave out and she collapsed into waiting arms.

The next few minutes were a blur. She was carried out

of the room with care Not knowing where they were taking her and what was going to happen next. Even though her eyes were closed, the sunlight that came through the open door seemed to burn through her eyelids. She didn't know where they were taking her, but she had no strength left to fight.

It wasn't until she smelled the reek of medications and antiseptic that she opened her eyes a little and saw she was in a moving ambulance.

"It's alright, Miss Finely. It's over. No one's going to hurt you. Just relax."

The gentle voice was soothing to her and for the first time since she'd been abducted, she felt safe. But it was an unusual feeling, a mistake, as though it was wrong to think she was safe. What if they were still out there? What if it was all part of the interrogation, psychological torture? Make her believe she was safe. Hope that she'd made it and then surprise her with the truth. Liz sat up and twisted her head, searching for the men. She struggled with the medics while yelling out for them to leave her alone.

"It's okay. You're safe," he assured her. Before she could react, the medic injected her with a sedative.

Liz opened her eyes and knew it was over. She was alone in a private room in a hospital. A drip was attached to her left hand and both wrists were bandaged. Just staring around the room made her feel dizzy. She closed her eyes holding her stomach, hoping not to throw up. While she waited for someone to enter, her mind replayed the attack. She couldn't fathom why she was still alive. Did she tell them what they wanted to know? Did she break and tell them everything? She couldn't remember. Her joy of being alive soon diminished as she remembered the torture, the pain from the shocks, the feeling of suffocation. Would she ever forget the smell? Her body jerked as though she'd been shocked again, and then the tears came.

She was still crying when a nurse entered the room. Pain medication and a light sedative soon took her away from the nightmare she was reliving.

She slept fitfully through the night, plagued with nightmares and panic. Twice she woke up dripping with sweat. Kicking off the soaked bedsheets, she managed to control her breathing and with time she calmed. Still weak with exhaustion, her eyes closed until the nightmares woke her again.

***

Alex didn't visit Liz until the following afternoon. He was told she wasn't allowed visitors, and he was questioned about his relationship with her. Liz thought he was deliberately staying away from her. However, he was the one who'd been ordered to evaluate her condition and report on how she was holding up. She'd received a visit by Hart, who informed her that the abduction was the last part of her training and that she was never in any real danger. He then gave her the good news about her qualifying as an agent.

Alex knew that the promotion could never make up for what she'd been put through. From the reports he'd heard, Liz had put up a good fight. Even at the end, when she thought she was dying, she just gave them her false name. He'd seen agents break after two rounds of the electric stun gun. The Water Boarding technique had only been used three times and never on a female. What did she do to make them press her so hard? Liz was a tough nut to crack. He hoped she'd be able to cope with the psychological aftermath. Alex knew agents that had come through the interrogation process but then fold due to psychological problems.

CHAPTER TWO
The Coded Mesage

Liz assumed Alex would have seen the tapes of her interrogation, but she wasn't prepared for the grimace on his face when he saw the damage.

"Jeez, you look a mess," he greeted.

"Yeah, well you should have seen the other guy," she replied with a tight smile.

Walking over to the side of the bed, he sat down on the mattress and couldn't take his eyes off the massive bruise that covered the left side of her face.

"How are you feeling?"

"Oh, you know, sore, aching, exhausted, as though I've just gone two rounds with Tyson."

"Yes. I do know. I've been through it. All agents have, but some don't make it."

"You ever lost one?" she asked, her anger getting the better of her. "I thought they were going to kill me, Alex. I thought I was dying. I couldn't breathe." Tears fell and her shoulders sagged as she broke down.

Alex shifted over and sat beside her allowing her head to rest on his chest while he stroked her hair. As she felt her body grow calm, Alex reached for Liz's hand and gently squeezed it.

"It's okay, honey. It's over," he whispered. "Did Hart tell you there's going to be an inquiry? They went too far." He growled.

"No, don't," she said and pulled herself into a sitting position. "I'm glad it was a setup. If it had been real, I don't think I'd be alive now. They were just following orders, doing their job like I thought I was. I don't bear any grudges, neither should you. Please get the inquiry dropped," she took his hand, "for me."

"If, you're sure. So, how are you sleeping? I know about the nightmares."

"I can't close my eyes without being back in that room. Promise me, Alex, promise it will get better."

"In time," he said. He held her until she pulled away.

"When are you seeing the shrink?"

"First session is tomorrow, but I don't think it's going to help. I just want to get out of here and get back to work. You know, get my mind off it."

"You need rest, Liz, or should that be Agent Finely?" He smiled.

"Does that mean I'm going to be working alongside you from now on?" she asked hopefully.

"Yes. We're going to be working closely together." He stared at her face and then glanced down at her lips, before cupping her chin. He lifted her head and gently kissed her lips.

It was more than a peck, more than a kiss of friendship, and both knew that.

"I'll be in to see you again, soon. Try to rest, Liz."

He stood up and stroked her head before turning to leave.

"I thought of you," she called out, stopping Alex from moving.

"When I was being interrogated, I thought about you. I assumed you'd come crashing through the door to rescue me." She smiled, and then looked down at her clasped hands. "I couldn't bear the thought of not seeing you again."

Alex turned and faced her. "I thought about it, believe me. If I'd known what they were going to do, I would have stopped it." Alex huffed. "Get some rest," he said sadly, and then left the room.

***

Liz wanted to prove to them that she was strong, that she wasn't traumatised by the incident. But she couldn't let go of the fact that if the abduction had been real, how much more torture would she have gone through? Would they have broken her? Would she be alive? Her imagination played the film of what could have happened: the pain, the screaming, the violence. It was hard to concentrate on anything else.

Although she'd been released from the clinic, she'd been ordered to stay home and rest. Five days laid up and no sign of when she was going to be allowed back to work. She felt caged and alone and wanted desperately to get back to the office, where she felt safe. The daily sessions with the therapist, in her opinion, were going nowhere. She just told him what he was sure he wanted to hear. The pain in her wrists and ankles had turned to a dull ache and the purple bruise was now a yellow tinge on her face. The last time Alex had visited, he'd brought with him her laptop. She hoped that surfing the net might keep her occupied.

****

Liz sat crossed-legged on the bed, her computer resting on the pillows. Once connected, she typed in the password to her email account. She knew there would be loads of spam emails waiting for her. The laptop was her personal computer, but she knew that when she returned to work certain security features would have to be installed and hopefully that would include the finest spam filter.

It didn't surprise her to see forty spam emails. There were four emails in her inbox. Knowing spam sometimes got through; she clicked on the inbox first. She deleted two of them without hesitation. One had To Make You Smile, from A, in the subject line. She knew who had sent it and so eagerly clicked on the mail. A poster of the cutest puppy took up the whole of the screen. She sighed, covered her heart with her hand, and after a minute of gazing, reluctantly deleted the mail. The last email caught her eye. For Your Eyes Only. It could have been an email advertising tablets that would give you a permanent erection, but something about it woke her curiosity. With two of the best virus protection software on her computer, she wasn't worried about clicking on it.

The email opened to reveal three separate lines of numbers. The numbers weren't in any apparent order, but they were separated into different blocks as though each block spelt out a word. It was a coded message, and someone wanted her to break it.

"When did you get this?" Alex asked as he scanned through the email.

"It was delivered two days ago, but I didn't open it until this afternoon."

"I'll need to take it in. Try to get an IP address on the sender and make sure you haven't released a tracer worm. I know just the person to give this to. He's a genius at cracking codes."

"Sure," she said, closing the lid of her laptop. "Do you mind if I work on it as well? It will give me something to do?"

"Yeah, good idea. You want me to send you a copy?"

"No. It's all in here," she said, pointing to her head.

"There's a reason it was sent to you," he smiled. "You're looking so much better. Animated, I would say. You were right when you said getting back to work would be beneficial for you.

"Yeah, my therapist said having something to do keeps my brain busy and the demons away."

Alex picked up the laptop and left as Liz started writing out the code.

Liz spent the evening and the following morning trying to work out the code. She broke it down, changed the numbers around, but nothing was jumping off the page. No matter, she wouldn't let it rest. And yet there was something familiar about the layout.

Was it another test from MI5? Maybe assessing to see if she could concentrate enough to solve it? Alex never gave her the impression that it was fake. However, she could say the same about his professionalism on the phony assignment, which had led to the horrific interrogation.

She quickly shook the thoughts away before they turned into graphic images again. A break, that's what she needed. Too paranoid to go for a walk, in case, she was under surveillance and got into trouble for disobeying orders, she moved away from the table where she'd been sitting for hours. Stretching her aching muscles, she then went into the kitchen to make a coffee. While waiting for the water to boil, she picked up a magazine and flicked through the pages. Her eyes landed on a page advertising a week on the beautiful island of Mykonos, Greece.

"Holy shit!"

Running through the kitchen and back into the lounge, she stared at the message again and it suddenly became clear.

***

Alex was in the boardroom in the middle of a meeting when Liz rushed inside.

"Agent Alex, I've solved it," she panted. Then glanced at the shocked and somewhat bemused faces of the rest of them in the room.

She coughed. "Sorry, but Agent Alex, you need to see this." She put the paper on the table and watched his expression turn from surprise to concern.

"I couldn't understand it at first, but then I remembered what you said about it had been sent to me for a reason."

Alex put a hand on her shoulder and started to steer her out of the office.

"Meeting's adjourned," he called back, before ushering her down the corridor.

In his office, he picked up the phone and made some

calls. Then Liz explained who had sent the email and how she was able to decipher the code.

Within ten minutes, the boardroom was full of the leading players of MI5.

Alex waited patiently until everyone was seated and then he began.

"Miss Finely received this email at 18.00 hours on Tuesday but didn't have the opportunity to open it until 14.00 hours on Friday."

The large white screen behind Alex displayed the numbered code for all to see.

"Mr West had been attempting to decipher the code but to no avail. The email was sent by anonymous email, and there is no way to trace the source. Although Miss Finely is not an authority code analyzer, she was able to decode the message."

The first slide vanished from the screen and was replaced by another. Whispers and intake of breath could be heard around the room.

"This may be a hoax, but because of the seriousness of what the message implies and to whom it was sent, I believe we should take the threat seriously."

All heads turned back to the screen; the message came up in bold capital black letters.

THERE IS A PLOT TO KIDNAP THE GREEK PRIME MINISTER AND HIS WIFE ON THEIR VISIT TO THE UK.

"Perhaps Miss Finely could inform us as to why the email was sent to her and what her involvement is in all this?" the director asked.

Liz stood up and faced her audience.

"The email was sent to me by my father, James Finley. I didn't discover this until I had translated the code. Let me explain. Although my father and I do not have a strong bond, one game we played, however now I know it was never a game." The director coughed.

"Yes, sorry, sir. He taught me how to leave messages in code. We came up with a disorganised alphabet. Each letter then represented a number, like so."

Liz clicked a button and the screen displayed large, jumbled letters of the alphabet. Starting at L and ending in D.

"It would be almost impossible or take a great deal of time for anyone to figure out this system. As far as I know, only my father and I know how to write and read this code."

"How do you think he's come across this information, Miss Finely? Who does your father work for?" Hart asked.

"I don't know, sir. I haven't spoken to my father in four years. The last I heard he was living in Greece."

More murmurs and quiet chatting, then the director cleared his throat.

"I think for the time being we should keep this in-house. No good causing the Greeks to panic when we have no solid evidence. Mr Soulanis is due to arrive in the UK next week. I don't see any reason for him to cancel his trip unnecessarily. Miss Finely, I want a full report on my desk as soon as possible, as well as a breakdown of this code."

"Yes, sir."

"Hart, see if you can locate Mr. Finely. Get in touch with our people over there and make sure he's under 24 hours surveillance. Mrs. Lyn, call your people and discreetly find out if there has been any talk or rumours flowing about. Janice, I want a list of active organizations that would be capable of pulling something like this off. I don't have to remind you all discretion is vital. We can't have this getting out before we have confirmation."

As the staff were filing out, the director called Alex back.

Liz sat at her desk and began writing down the key to unlock the code. She was ten when her father taught her the game. Even at that age, she was soaking up information. She felt a presence beside her and turned to see Alex glaring at her.

"How did he know you worked for the Secret Service?" he asked. She didn't think it was said as an accusation. All the same, she noted his serious tone.

"I have no idea. I swear to you, I haven't told anyone. Who's there to tell? I never had friends back at my old place and I told you, I haven't spoken to my dad in nearly four years. And even then, it was just a quick phone call. He just upped and left after my mother died. Any relationship we had was broken when he left me. I didn't know he was in Greece until you'd brought me in that time and read out my file. You do believe me, don't you?" She stared hard at him, trying to read what he was thinking.

"Of course, I do. But that just leaves the question who does your father work for?" He touched her lightly on the shoulder. "Don't think about this now. You'd better get the report finished. Jack's waiting."

Alex left her to concentrate, but how could she? Her father had decided to enter her life again bringing with him a shit load of trouble. She'd never been particularly close to him and couldn't remember ever having a father and daughter heart-to-heart. She knew her mother's death destroyed him, but that did not give him the right to just walk out without a word of goodbye. He could have been dead, but she knew he was still alive. What an entrance to make. Who was he working for and where did he get the intel? More importantly, would he contact her again? No matter what happened now, she was in deep, and it would be up to her to resolve the crisis. The huge weight she had on her shoulders tugged on her muscles and rubbing did not ease the dull ache.

Sighing, she looked down at the paperwork and began writing again.

***

The weekend passed fast and on Monday morning Liz was just about to step into the Thames building when her mobile rang.

"Liz, you'd better get here quick. We have a situation," Alex said.

"I'm on my way up," she said, pushing through the doors.

She rushed up to the 2nd floor and walked into chaos. There was an operator on every computer monitor, diligently tapping away on the keyboards. A glass screen covered the back wall, displaying a blue detailed map of the towns and streets in Athens. Red dots signified the hot spots. People were rushing around everywhere; phones were ringing, and a man was barking out orders. West was rushing past her, hugging files to his chest when she grabbed his arm.

"What's going on?" she asked.

"Two Greek dignitaries have been assassinated," he said, before rushing off.

"Agent Finley, over here."

She turned to see Alex waving her over and then followed him into his office.

"There were two separate car bombings in Athens early this morning. Both were members of the Greek cabinet. Both were killed. We think it's related to the planned kidnapping. No one has accepted responsibility for the bombings. The Greeks have started leaning on known terrorist groups."

"Do you think the politicians were involved in the threat?" she asked.

"Nothing's been confirmed. But we're not ruling out the possibilities that they could have been. Maybe word of our involvement has gotten out, and they're killing off anyone who's involved."

Seating himself behind the desk, he signalled for Liz to sit down.

"I thought this was supposed to be kept in-house."

Alex raised his eyebrows. She understood.

"Have we any new intel?" she asked.

"There are a few possible suspects, but at the moment nothing has been confirmed. We need evidence and testimonies. That's where you come in."

She leaned in closer.

"Jack wants you to send a coded email to your father and request that you meet."

"I see."

"I know it's asking a lot from you, putting you out there again after what's just happened. But no one else can do this. It has to be you. I doubt James will want to speak to anyone else. You need to meet with him and get confirmation. We need to know dates, names everything." He stopped to see her reaction. "Do you think you're up for it? There's no one else, but if push comes to shove, we'll have to find another way. Hart doesn't think you're ready to go back in the field, mainly because of your lack of experience and because of the risk factor involved. It could be dangerous, Liz."

She sat up straight in the chair. "I'm ready. I feel like I've been waiting forever for a chance like this. I won't let you down."

Alex nodded.

"You know, if he's working for the other side, it's doubtful he'll open up to me. Our relationship is strained, and we weren't that close, to begin with."

"But close enough for him to contact you. I think he wants to meet you face-to-face. He has more to say, I'm sure of it."

"You think he's working as a double agent?" she asked.

"I'm not sure what to think, Liz. First things first; you need to send him an email, tell him you're going to be in Athens tomorrow morning, and you want to meet. I've booked you a ticket on Olympic airlines, you depart at 7 am. Hart wants to brief you before you leave. Right now, you need to read up on the intel we have. Everything you need to know is in these files. Call me if you need me."

Liz spent the next few hours reading through the informative intel MI5 had on four known terrorist groups.

First, there was Black Star: as their attacks were marked on embassies and diplomats, it put them at the top of the list. This group was anti-establishment, anti-government. Most of their previous demands were for the release of political prisoners.

She chewed on the lid of the pen she held as she continued to read through the documents, trying to memorize all the names and alias. Liz was surprised any terrorist groups were working in Greece. She'd never heard of any attacks or bombings, but then again, if she had, it wouldn't have bothered her. But things had changed and now she needed to know about everything and everyone in the organisations.

The most notorious group known in Greece was the Revolutionary Organization – 17 November also known as 17N or N17. A far-left group, it was responsible for most car bombings and terrorist activity in Greece. However, the group was disbanded in 2002 after the main leaders were arrested and charged with over a thousand counts of terrorism.

Revolutionary Struggle was formed after the break of N17. This group targeted embassies and political buildings and were responsible for the rocket launched at the US Embassy in Greece in 2005.

The last group: Revolutionary Nuclei was a small group with few members and according to the file, no longer active.

It was unlikely N17 had enough members or finance to pull off a kidnapping in the UK. But wouldn't that be the perfect ploy, to be underground, combining their efforts and resources and then come above ground most spectacularly, by killing or kidnapping the Greek Prime Minister. Liz tapped the pen lid on her teeth as she thought hard. *But who could they have joined forces with? Who has that much power in Greece?* The mafia came to mind, but Liz didn't even know if there was a Greek mafia. There was no mention of the organization in the files she was reading. *So, either one of the groups has re-formed and combined their efforts and resources, or there's a new threat in Greece,*

Liz also spent time researching possible organizations that her father might be involved in. *How did he come by the information, who is he working for?* Liz poured out another black coffee from the fast-emptying percolator jug. She felt tired and stressed and hoped the caffeine would help.

Who was this man? She couldn't imagine him being involved in an assassination or a plot to kidnap, but then again, she was now working for the British Secret Service. Something she would never have thought about five years ago.

The meeting with Hart was short. He told her that there would be two more agents on the flight with her and then they'd be met at the airport by Greek Intelligence. Hart made her assignment sound easy. Meet up with Finely, find out who's involved with the kidnapping and when and where it was supposed to take place. Find out who Finely was working for and how he heard about the plan.

But Liz knew it wasn't going to be that simple. There was bound to be word out that British Intelligence was arriving in Athens. And her father was putting himself and her at risk by meeting. Liz didn't know what to expect, and it was that which caused the chill to creep up her arm.

***

On the journey down to the airport, Alex and the other agents went through possible scenarios with her and then tested the tracking device. She put the micro recorder in her jacket pocket. Not wanting to cause unnecessary attention, the agents were casually dressed. Even then they stood out, she thought, carrying an air of authority with them as though they were someone special.

Liz loved the way Alex looked when he dressed down. He appeared more relaxed than the suited agent she worked within the office. He was dressed in jeans and a blue sweatshirt and dark sunglasses. She sat in the passenger's seat, beside him as he drove the black Range Rover. She had a hard time keeping her eyes diverted. She wanted to wear jeans, but Alex insisted on black trousers and a cream top. A small fitted grey jacket finished off the ensemble. The small luggage case she had, contained a suit for official meetings, another change of clothes, sleeping apparel just in case it was going to be an overnight stay, and the essentials a woman would need to keep up her appearance.

She felt she was back in school as he instructed her on protocol and the assignment like she hadn't heard it before. Her head was buzzing by the time they reached Heathrow airport. Remembering that he was still her supervisor, she stopped herself from telling him to shut up. He was just being careful, but it made her feel as though he didn't have confidence in her. Assuring him that she knew her role and that she would call in every two hours, she then followed the two agents onto the aircraft and settled in for the three-and-a-half-hour flight.

Liz had never flown first-class before, so the experience was a little exciting. Determined to enjoy the pampering, she nestled into the seat and watched the blue sky replace the green scenery. Feeling relaxed and sleepy as she lounged in the black leather chair, she waited until the plane had levelled out. She was tired and knew she should stay awake and should have ordered a double expresso, but her eyes closed, and her body was grateful for the respite.

An hour and a half later, she woke to the sound of the captain's voice announcing the altitude of the plane and the weather in Athens. She left her seat and walked up and down the plane to stretch her legs. The stewardess was serving drinks when she arrived back. She ordered a Coke and then took out her laptop to study the intel again. Once connected, a message popped up informing her she had mail. Liz took out her note pad and pen when she realised it was another coded email.

Her heartbeat fast, and her pulse raced as the numbers became words. Shifting in her chair, she glanced over at the other agents to make sure they weren't watching. Staring at the message, she gulped as she considered the implication.

MEET ME OUTSIDE OF DEPARTURES. LOSE THE OTHERS.

CHAPTER THREE
The Chase

The first thought that came into her head was that it might not be her father who was sending the messages. He could be under due arrest and have been tortured into giving them the code. She squeezed her eyes shut at the memory of her torture. It could be a trap and meeting the contact unarmed and without backup would be a serious mistake. But what else could she do? She'd been instructed to come alone. If she didn't comply it would be unlikely that she'd get the information they needed.

"You got another one, agent Finely?" a voice asked, making her jump.

Liz turned to the agent and smiled tightly. "Yes. It says I'm going to be contacted again, at 1pm, Greek time."

"Good," he replied. "I'll inform headquarters."

She hated lying to her colleagues. Sweat formed on her top lip, and she quickly wiped it away. What she was doing was wrong. They wouldn't understand. She knew there would be trouble when she got back to the UK, and how was she supposed to get to departures without the dogs following?

"Hart wants you to forward the email," the agent said after taking on the phone.

"Right away," she announced.

It would take West only a few minutes to decipher the message and then what? The agents would be told to follow her undetected. She couldn't risk it. But what if headquarters called back to say they hadn't received the message. How long would they wait? It was a chance she was willing to take. Her finger hovered over the send button. She then closed the lid of the laptop, sipped her drink wishing it was a whisky and Coke instead. She needed something to take the edge off.

Liz breathed a sigh of relief when they touched down in Athens. Even though she'd made her decision on how to proceed, there were still doubts. Her only doorway of escape was between passing customs and before she met with the Greek officials.

"I need a quick toilet break," she announced. "I'll be back in a minute. Look after this for me."

She left the agents with her luggage and walked down the wide shopping arcade, then turned left, out of sight. Liz located the lifts and then pressed the button for departures.

There was no going back now, she told her pounding heart. The doors opened. She took one step out of the lift and glanced both ways before walking out. The lounge was full, and it would be hard to spot anyone in the crowd. She dodged luggage trolleys and passed by travellers who appeared bewildered. Liz didn't have the time to waste searching for the exit and so she walked over to the nearest flight representative and asked for directions in Greek. Her enunciation was very fluid, and the man didn't have a problem understanding her. He pointed to the left and told her it was at the top.

"Σας ευχαριστώ." (Thank you.)

Liz walked briskly away. She was happy to make it outside for some silence and fresh air.

She'd only been waiting outside for about a minute when a battered, white Ford escort pulled up. The driver pulled down the window and shouted for her to get in. Although she didn't recognise him, there was no mistaking her father's voice.

Relieved, she opened the door and stepped into the car. There was barely enough time to shut the door before the car sped away.

Liz turned her head and stared at her father. The long brown beard and scraggly, unwashed hair added years on him. Dressed in baggy brown corduroys and a green pullover, she hoped it was a disguise and not the normal way he now dressed.

Tongue-tied, she didn't know what to say to him.

"You're looking well," he said. His sight remained on the road as they exited the airport and started down the motorway.

"What's going on, Dad?"

"I would never have imagined you'd be working for the Secret Service," he said, ignoring her question.

"How did you find out?" she asked.

He turned his head toward her. "Are you recording this conversation?"

"Yes." It was no good lying to him. He was more astute than she gave him credit for.

"Turn it off," he said, and then faced the road again.

As Liz did what she was told, she glanced in the side mirror.

"We have company," she said.

"Yours or mine?"

"They're not mine. They don't know I'm missing yet."

"Okay, hold on," he said

Without hesitation, Liz grabbed and fastened her seatbelt as James increased his speed. Horns were thumped angrily, and tyres screeched as he swerved past traffic.

"So, are you going to tell me what's going on? Who are you working for?"

"All in good time," he smiled, then patted her knee. She nearly grabbed hold of the steering wheel, afraid that he'd crash the car driving one-handed.

He was a skilled driver. It wasn't the first time he'd been involved in a car chase, she mused, as she watched him dodging traffic and then turning into back roads. Within ten minutes they'd lost the tail.

James pulled up in a small street and told her to get out. Beside the car was a Suzuki 250 motorbike. He took a key out of his pocket and then threw her a helmet.

"Easier to get away from trouble," he grinned.

Liz climbed on the back and held on to her father as he put the key in the ignition and opened the throttle.

She watched the landscape whiz by as she held on tightly. She'd never been to Greece before and even though it wasn't a sightseeing tour, she managed to get a glimpse of the famous Acropolis. They left Athens and headed for Megara. Before she left the UK, Liz had spent time looking through maps of Greece, wanting to familiarize herself with the names of towns and rivers.

As they entered Korinthos, a beach resort, James slowed down the bike and came to a stop outside a quaint Taverna called Kipos (The Garden). There were no customers, so Liz had a choice of where she wanted to sit. For late summer, the day was warm and as siesta time was coming up, the hottest part of the day, she chose a table shaded by a large orange umbrella advertising some orange juice.

The waiter came over and greeted them with a smile.

James was ordering a kilo of house white when Liz interrupted.

"Συγνώμη. Ένα ποτήρι κόκκινο κρασί παρακαλώ."

(Sorry, one glass of red wine please.)

"Your Greek is good," her dad said, surprised.

"I don't like white wine, and I shouldn't even be drinking when I'm on duty. So, one glass is more than enough."

He frowned and then lowered his eyes to the menu before choosing stuffed tomatoes, feta cheese and Greek salad for two. The waiter took his order and then left them alone.

"I'm not hungry," she said.

"You could at least try the Greek cuisine while you're here," he smiled.

Liz could tell that her father was enjoying the situation, but she had no intention of dropping her guard. "It's nice to see you again, Elizabeth."

"This isn't a social visit, so cut the crap." She snapped.

James didn't speak again until the waiter had brought the drinks.

"So, what do you want to know?" He asked.

"First off, how did you find me?"

"I didn't have to find you," he said, "I always knew

where you were. Is it wrong to keep tabs on a daughter?"

To know that her father had been watching her, gave her chills and she needed to know why?

"Why didn't you get in touch? Pick up the phone or something? Instead of spying on me."

"It's not as easy as you make it sound," he replied. "Now let me ask you a question? Why MI5? What happened to your singing?"

"I met a man, and he changed my life," she shrugged.

"Do you love him?"

She didn't answer.

"Liz don't ever fall in love with a spy. It's the worst mistake you can make."

"What the hell do you know about it?" she retorted.

Liz was shocked by the sudden change in his face, the sadness his eyes portrayed as though he was fighting a distant memory he'd hoped to forget.

"I never told you about your mother," he said.

Before she could question him further, the waiter appeared with the food. He took his time putting the plates on the table. Liz wished he would leave so she could talk to her father again. Why mention her mother? Why had the conversation suddenly turned personal?

"What about Mum?" she asked the moment the waiter was out of earshot.

"She wasn't killed in a car crash. She was murdered."

The world stood still as his words bounced around her head while she tried to make sense of it.

"Murdered! By whom?" she whispered.

"That's what I've been trying to find out." James took a forkful of feta and raised it to his mouth, then paused.

"Your mum worked for the government, some covert operation. No one knew about it. She didn't exist." He watched Liz's face pale, before putting the fork into his mouth.

"What branch of the government? How come I never knew?" she cried.

"How could you? She was good at living a lie. The government covered it up. But I knew the truth. I know what she was doing the day she died. She was going to warn a target about an assassination attempt. I tried to stop her, but I just didn't try hard enough."

Pushing away his plate, he bowed his head. "I loved her so much. We knew our relationship was dangerous, but we couldn't let go. That's why I left. I knew they'd be looking for me and you'd be in danger. It was better if I wasn't around."

Liz was silent. She couldn't believe what he was saying. Her mother, an agent, and her father – what was her father? Who did he work for?

"Who's looking for you?"

"It doesn't matter," he replied and took a sip of wine. "Eat something, will you? You're wasting away."

Liz picked at her food, but the little appetite she had was lost.

There was much more she wanted to ask, but her assignment took precedence.

"What do you know about the plot to kidnap Vasilis Soulanis? Who's involved? Where's it going to take place?"

She ate a mouthful of food, just to please him. The rice was creamy, and the tomatoes were succulent. She washed it down with a swig of wine, never taking her eyes off him.

"It's not a kidnapping. There's going to be an assassination on Soulanis while he's in the UK. There are no specifics, but there's a lot of movement going on and members of the group are already in the UK preparing. They could hit a convoy, blow up the hotel he's staying at, or just shoot him on one of his planned walks about. No one's talking, but they have the means and funding to pull off anything. It's not what you think. N17 are not involved," he said, as though reading her mind, "but it's going to appear as though they are. I'm assuming they are your main concern?"

Liz nodded.

"Forget it. Look elsewhere. But you'll need to dig hard. These guys are unknown, not that they haven't been around for a while."

"What do they call themselves?" she asked.

"A.G.C. Against Government Corruption. They want to change government policy. They think the public has a right to control their country."

"How come we've never heard of them before? You say they've been around a while."

"They are careful. They've made their presence known, but never taken responsibility."

"And now?"

Liz took a sip of her wine and then picked at the salad. The Greek salad was the best thing she'd ever tasted. The olive oil was rich and silky on the tongue. She wiped away the juice from the cucumber as it dripped down her chin.

"They've been planning for this a long time." He continued, "The attack will not be expected. They are not afraid to kill and die while trying."

As if he could read her mind, he quickly added, "Cancel the visit and there will be serious repercussions."

"You're part of this group?" she cried, slamming her folk down onto the table.

"No, I'm bloody not! And don't you dare raise your voice at me again. Show some respect!" He sighed and breathed out loudly and talked softly to her. "Do you think I'd be talking to you now if I was part of their group?"

"Then how do you know everything? Who told you?"

"Let's just say I heard it through the grapevine. I'm not giving you names, if that's what you're going to ask next. You should be more worried about where the original leak came from."

"What do you mean?"

He leaned over towards her and put his hand on top of hers. "Who do you trust in MI5?"

Liz didn't grasp the context at first. "I don't know my colleagues well yet, but I trust them."

"Yes, but who can you trust?" he said, and then sat back in his chair with a smirk.

"Are you saying that the original leak about the planned assassination came from MI5?"

He nodded.

"No way. I don't believe it. That's saying one of us is involved."

"Believe it, honey. I wish I could tell you the name of the informant, but I don't know who he - she is. That's why I contacted you. I thought you should know you have a mole in your organisation."

Liz didn't know what to say next. The thought that someone in her organisation was a mole, a traitor, was very disturbing. *Who could it be? And who can I trust to tell what I've learnt? There was only one man, Alex.*

"So, what do you do now?" James asked, after giving her time to think.

"I'll go back to the UK, tell Mr Jones what I know. He's the only one I can trust. I just hope I don't get fired for not following protocol."

James shook his head. "They wouldn't do that. You're too important to them."

"Yeah, thanks to you." she smiled slightly. "Can you keep your ears to the ground and let me know if you hear of anything new, dates, time, etc.? We're going to have to smoke the mole out. Contact me if you hear of any movement from MI5."

"Sure, but you'll have to use a public connection. They're bound to put tabs on your computer. I'll use swan as my email address."

She felt a sudden pain in her chest, and tears threatened to fall. "That's what you used to call Mum."

"It was until they clipped her wings," he said sadly.

"So, what was she, some sort of agent?"

"I've told you as much as I know. She worked for a hushed-up branch of the government. She wouldn't talk about her work. She was very secretive."

Liz thought back to when she was younger. "I remember her being away a lot. In fact, I remember you being away as well. Mum said you were travelling because of work. We didn't have a lot of time together as a family."

"Yes, but the times we had together were magical."

Liz turned away from her dad and tried to concentrate on watching passers-by. Three to a moped, an old Greek woman dressed in black, pulling a donkey overloaded with black nets that were used to catch the olives that fell from the trees. But it was the sight of a little blonde girl who walked past holding hands with her mother, which caused her childhood memories to flashback images of the good times they shared.

"You don't work for a branch of the government. It's obvious you're anti-establishment. So, who do you work for?" she snapped, angry for allowing her emotions to get the better of her.

"I work for myself," he said. "If you weren't with the Secret Service, I'd tell you. Better to let sleeping dogs lie. It's safer if you don't know. Trust me on this."

But she couldn't let it rest. Something was niggling in the back of her mind.

"Have you ever killed anyone?" she asked.

James paused before replying "Yes, on more than one occasion. Have you?"

"No. I've fired a gun, but I've never shot at anyone."

"You will," he said, then took out his wallet and threw thirty euros on the table before picking up his helmet.

"So, where to?" he asked.

"Drop me off at the nearest hotel. I can't go to the one I'm booked in. I'm in some serious shit, thanks to you, and I need to think about how I'm going to proceed before I contact headquarters."

"I still can't get over the fact that you work for MI5. I thought I taught you better than that," he growled.

She could sense his anger. But she felt it was more than just her working for the government. The way he glared at her and snapped and got angry. She felt she didn't know who the person was anymore. There was no closeness or family vibes between them, and Liz got an awful suspicion that he was keeping something big from her. He'd always had his secrets, but she never questioned his actions until now.

They left the tavern and climbed back onto the bike. James headed north, and after a few minutes, parked outside Hotel Paradise. Taking his helmet off he turned to Liz with a serious expression etched on his face.

"I'm sure you will hear from me again soon. But if you don't. Just know I love you and I hope you forgive me."

There was nothing left to say, so she just nodded.

"Oh, and Elizabeth. Don't trust anyone. Things are not what they seem." He winked before putting his helmet on and speeding away.

Forgive him for what? What has he done, or what is he planning to do and what did he mean by things are not what they seem? Am I being played by my own government or by my father? Liz rubbed her aching forehead and cursed herself for drinking the wine.

***

Opening the door to her room, she threw herself on the bed. This time she allowed the tears to come. Her mother had worked for a special ops team and had been murdered and they covered it up, why? And although James had been vague about what he did, she had an idea, and the thought chilled her.

Her past life felt like a dream. Nothing was real. Both of her parents had lived a lie and now she was living the nightmare. She felt exhausted in mind and body.

Walking into the small, simple white bathroom, complimentary soaps and shampoos, and fluffy white bath towels greeted her. Having left her luggage at the airport with the officers, she didn't have a change of clothes but at least she could shower and wash her hair, she thought thankfully.

After towel drying her hair, she tied it up in a ponytail. Without a comb, her hair was going to dry curly, and she knew she was going to look like a scarecrow in the morning, but there was nothing to be done.

She'd barely eaten anything and even though her stomach rumbled for food, she knew that with her nerves, she wouldn't be able to keep anything in.

Knowing she couldn't keep her eyes open anymore, but not sure if her mind would turn off long enough to fall asleep, she pulled back the white cotton sheets and got into bed.

Liz was woken by a knock on the door. Wondering why the proprietor or cleaner would be bothering her at 3'oclock in the morning, she got out of bed, wrapped the sheet around her body and switched the light on before opening the door. She was startled to see Alex standing outside.

"What are you doing here?" she cried.

Ignoring her, he barged past her and entered her room.

"What the fuck are you playing at?" he yelled as he held her shoulders and shook her.

Liz, stunned by his actions, pushed him off and stepped away.

"You know the trouble you've caused? We had the Greek Police searching the airport for hours. You can't just disappear without telling anyone." He walked slowly over to her, and this time gently put his hand on her shoulder.

"Anything could have happened. I thought you'd been abducted."

"I'm sorry, Alex, but I had no choice. Please sit down and I'll explain."

Alex sat down on a chair beside the dressing mirror, while she sat on the edge of the bed and faced him.

She told him everything.

He didn't stop and question her. Even though his mouth didn't move, his eyes were watching her carefully, reading her to see if she was telling the truth, studying her emotions.

"And you have all this on the micro-recorder," he asked, after she finished.

"No, I don't. He made me switch it off."

Alex shook his head, disappointed. "Typical!" he growled.

"But I had a backup." She smiled. "I tried to record only the intel we needed, but my mother is mentioned. Is there any way we can edit it before handing it over?"

"Sorry, Liz, but the disk is going to be examined, and they'll know if it's been tampered with."

"I don't want them to know about my mother," she cried. "I don't want them to know I know. Do you know how it will make me appear? Especially now, with my father somehow knowing about the plot on the Greek prime minister.

Alex stood up and sat on the bed beside her. He pulled her to him and kissed the top of her head.

"A spy, a double agent. But I know that's not you. I've known you for a while now. I know your character. Okay, I'm going to do some digging, see if I can find anything relating to your mother's work. But if the branch was as secret as you say it is, I'm likely to come up blank."

"Thank you. I know I can't bring her back; I just need to know who my mum was."

"What about your dad?"

"He didn't tell me a lot."

Alex lifted her chin. "But he told you enough. Go with your gut instinct. What's your first thought?"

Liz sighed and turned her head away. "He's hiding something. He fed me little bites that wouldn't lead to much but enough to cause noise within MI5. Honestly, he could be a hired assassin for all I know. I think Mum might have been going to warn one of his targets."

Alex stood up and grabbed his hair. "Hell! If word of this gets out, you'll be out of a job."

She stared at the threadbare carpet and nodded. "Oh, Alex, what am I going to do?"

He sat down beside her and pulled her to him. Then Alex raised his hand and gently brushed her tears away. He bought her face up to his and stared at her lips before looking into her eyes.

Clutching the back of her neck, he pulled her to him and kissed her passionately. So caught off guard, it took a moment before she kissed him back. The hairs on her arms rose, and an intense shiver rippled through her body. Tugging off his t-shirt, she stroked the soft skin of his back and sucked on his neck.

He groaned as he unwrapped the sheet from around her and stared at her almost naked body. He fumbled with the bra clip, finally getting it undone. Taking the straps off her, he threw the bra over his shoulder before his head bent and he devoured her breasts. Liz's hands were shaking as she undid his belt buckle. Alex moved away and stood up as he quickly undressed. He threw the bedsheet and laid on the bed naked, waiting for Liz to join him.

The sex was hot and fast and left them both satisfied, but breathless. She wondered how long it had been since he'd made love. Had he been waiting as long as she had?

Alex laid his head on her chest while Liz played with his hair.

It was the first time she'd seen that side of Alex, relaxed and happy away from the office and stress of leading a double life, Liz felt she didn't need to hide behind lies and protocol. For now, she could be herself and enjoy the time they had together. Even so, she couldn't forget the threat that faced her when she returned.

They had sex again, but not having a second condom, Alex pulled out and came on her stomach. After they showered off the sweat and cum, they got back into bed and Liz tried to relax.

"Do you think Jack will be lenient with me when he knows everything?"

"I'll smooth things over. But you should have told me what you were planning to do."

"I'm sorry." She turned her head and faced him. "Umm by the way, how the hell did you find me?"

"The transmitter."

"Shit! I forgot all about that." She inwardly laughed at her stupidity. "So, who do you trust in MI5? Who do we give the intel to?

"I trust Jack with my life. I'll let him listen to the orig-inal first. He'll have to edit the part about an informer in

MI5, so he may as well take out the part about your mother. That way the others will only listen to what they need to hear."

She sat up and rested her arm on his chest and stared into Alex's face. "Do you think he'll do that?"

"Yes. Hart will want to listen to the tape himself, but Jack will stall him. It's better if he keeps the original just in case."

"I hope so. So, you're going to tell Jack about the mole?"

"That's the first thing I'm going to tell him."

"And you trust him?"

"Yes."

She didn't need to ask why. She had put her trust in Alex and if he had trust in Jack, well that was good enough for her.

Reaching over to the phone, Alex called down to reception and asked if it was possible to have some food brought up, but apparently, the kitchen was closed.

"You hungry?" he asked.

"Starving. Suddenly I have an appetite. Must be the workout." She winked.

"I'll go out and see if I can find us some supper."

She grinned as she watched him dress and then leave the room.

Feeling fulfilled in more ways than one, exhaustion overtook hunger, and she closed her eyes.

***

Liz bolted up in bed as a noise woke her. A dark figure stood at the end of the bed, and she knew it wasn't Alex.

Before the assailant had time to raise his gun, she rolled

to the left of the bed and threw herself onto the floor.

The bullet shattered the lamp on the bedside table. A large piece of ceramic hit her left arm.

She knew the wise thing to do would be to leap over the bed to the door and try to escape, with only a bleeding arm, but instead, she leapt onto the bed and launched herself at the gunman.

Ramming her right elbow into the guy's jaw, she grabbed for the gun and struggled with him, but he was too strong.

He threw her to the floor and sat on her stomach as they both wrestled with the gun. He pushed the cold tip of the silencer against her naked waist.

She struggled with him as he started to squeeze the trigger, pushing against his strength to get the gun away from her body.

As the gun went off, Alex came crashing through the door.

Liz watched the gunman jump to his feet and rush at Alex, and then her vision blurred and all she saw was darkness.

***

Liz woke to find Alex sitting beside her hospital bed, holding her hand.

"How are you doing?" he asked.

A day's growth of stubble couldn't cover the sadness etched on his face, she thought. Her tongue stuck to the roof of her mouth. She was parched. As she tried to reach for a glass of water, Alex pushed her gently back down onto the bed. She winced from the pain that shot through her body. Alex reached over for the glass and noticing her shaking hands, held the glass to her lips while she drank.

The water tasted wonderful, cold, and wet, just what she needed. Alex moved the glass away and then smiled.

"Did you get him?" Liz asked.

Alex shook his head.

"Did you recognize who it was?" he asked.

"No, it was too dark."

"Look, Liz, you can't go home. You're gonna have to stay in a hotel after you're released from here. I have guards stationed outside the door."

"Why? What's going on?"

"After the hit on you…"

"What makes you think it was a hit?" she interrupted.

Alex stood up and leaned in closer. "There's a contract out on you," he whispered, "and we don't know why."

She gasped. He continued.

"By the time I could get help, you'd lost too much blood and so while you were still out, I had you flown back to the UK. You're in – Royal Infirmary. Only our team and your father knew which hotel you were in."

"Maybe I was followed?"

Alex raised his eyebrows. "Were you?"

"No," she answered." I was keeping a watch."

He nodded. "Exactly. So, there must have been a leak coming from the inside. Only those in the office knew about the tracking device. Only a few knew about which hotel you were in."

"I guess that doesn't leave too many suspects. But why put a hit on me? Do you think it's because of my dad?"

"That's not all," Alex said not answering her question. "After you were settled and out of danger, I went back to your apartment and swept it for bugs. Liz, you were riddled. Someone's been keeping surveillance on you. I'm guessing ever since you moved into the place."

She shook her head. "That's impossible. The place gets swept regularly. You know that."

"Yes. But by whom?"

"Shit! What kind of surveillance?" She stared into his face. "What did you find, Alex?"

Alex sat on the edge of her bed before answering. "Thirteen bugs and three cameras."

"Oh my God," she cried as she covered her face with her hands.

Alex put his arm around her. "We can't use a safe house as they have been compromised. We think it's best if you stay in a hotel for a while."

"Who's we? Who have you told?"

"Just Hart and Jack."

"And you trust them?"

Alex nodded. "Your location has to stay between the four of us. As far as anyone in the office knows, you're still in critical condition. No one is allowed to see you, except me." Alex started pacing the room.

"Hell, Liz, even I don't know who to trust anymore."

"I hope we've done the right thing in trusting Hart."

"You'll be here for a few more days. Take this time to rest. You look as though you need it." He smiled and then stood up and put his jacket on.

"You're leaving?"

"I have to. There's a lot that needs arranging. Don't worry it's unlikely I'd forget you." Bending over he kissed her cheek even though her lips were puckered.

"So, it's back to business, is it?" She moaned. Folding her arms across her chest, she glared hard.

"I think it's for the best. Don't you?"

Liz shrugged. "Yeah, I supposed so."

"At least for now." He smiled and then turned and left the room.

***

Now alone and there being silence, Liz went over the situation in her head. *Who is the traitor? Who has the contract out on me? Is it to do with my father, mother, or the planned attack on the Greek President? Could my father really be a hired assassin? No, I know we're not close, but there's no reason for him to put a hit out on me. No reason at all.* Her mind went back to the room, it slowly played the sequences of what happened as she searched her memory for any clues, anything she missed at the time, only she came up empty. One thing she did know, was that the man was hired by someone to kill her. *What had her father told her to put her life in jeopardy? Which side does he work for?* She didn't sleep as those thoughts and others filled her head.

Alex didn't visit until the following evening. He'd shaved but still looked exhausted, she thought.

Small talk was made, but most of his visit was spent in silence, uncomfortable silence. Alex then mentioned that he and Hart were going to let it slip that she was now conscious, out of danger and going to be moved to a safe house.

"That way we can flush the spy out," he said.

"So, once you know who it is, can I go back to my place?" she asked.

"No, even then you won't be safe."

She sighed.

"I'm gonna take your stuff with me now, and I'll bring you some new clothing tomorrow. The doctor said you can be released, but you need total bed rest. I'm having a friend stay at the hotel with you."

"An agent?

"No. All she knows is you're a friend of mine that needs some care. She's a qualified nurse. At least she'll be able to make sure you do as your told." He smiled.

"Yeah, but isn't it risky putting your friend in this situation?"

"More of a risk if I told her the truth," he answered. "Get some rest. I'll be back to collect you tomorrow."

"You too," she said. "You look bloody awful."

Alex smiled tightly before leaving the room.

***

Many days passed and Liz sat bored in the hotel room, unable to leave and unable to get any intel on what was happening, as Alex hadn't visited since they settled her in the hotel. All she had for company was her laptop and a TV and the nurse who wasn't talkative and Liz made sure she didn't say too much either. She watched the news that day and it talked about the coming visit of the Greek Prime minister. Liz wondered what security precautions they had put in effect and if they had told the Greeks about the shooting.

The following morning Liz was woken up early by a knock on the door. She got out of bed, wrapped the complimentary bathrobe around her and slowly open the door a crack to see who was there.

"Alex," she called out in surprise and opened the door. Poking her head around into the corridor, she noticed security was no longer outside.

Alex answered her question before she had a chance to ask.

"It's over, we found the mole. It was Katie, I don't think you knew her well. We've got intel on who she's been working for."

"Who?" Liz asked.

"That's classified on a need-to-know basis and I'm sorry, but you don't need to know."

"So, I'm the one who told you about the leak and that you had a traitor in MI5. I'm the one who has a contract on my head. I'm the one who got shot. I could have been killed and you tell me it's classified, and I don't need to know why it happened and who orchestrated." Liz glared at him. "What the fuck, Alex?"

Alex shrugged and glanced down at his feet rather than look her in the eye.

Did they not trust me anymore?

"So, I can leave this room at last?" she asked.

"Yep, you can go back home. The apartment is clean. I've made sure of it."

Liz left out a long sigh. "Thank God. I don't think I could have stayed in the room any longer. Give me fresh air for fuck's sake."

Alex laughed. "Come on I have a car waiting to take you home."

In the car, Liz broke the silence. "You said it wasn't safe for me to go back home and now it's okay. What's changed and don't give me that classified bullshit?"

Alex didn't answer her.

Liz sighed. "After everything that has happened, do I still have a job?"

"Of course!" Alex said. "We need you, you're part of the team, your skills are needed. Why would they fire you when you've done nothing wrong?"

Liz raised her eyebrows. "If I've done nothing wrong, why am I being kept from information, which I'm certain concerns me. I'm not fucking stupid, Alex. Don't underestimate me!"

Liz turned her head and stared out of the window at the grey rainy miserable day. Just how she felt inside – miserable. And the tears she wanted to shed, like the rain that fell outside. She held back. Wanting to give the impression that she was strong and yet she felt everything in her life was falling apart and she didn't know why.

"Maybe you haven't quite followed the rules," Alex spoke. "But everything has turned out okay and we got the mole. Without you, we wouldn't have even known about the leak."

Yeah, but you're still keeping the truth from me.

Liz bit her lip. "So, what happens next?"

"Well, we have the Greek Prime Minister's visit to arrange. As you know the assassination plot is still happening, and we need to take precautions. I'll get you up to date tomorrow at the office. Just take today to rest and come up with some suggestions and ideas on how and where the assassination could take place."

"Will do," she answered.

The car pulled up outside her apartment. The two said their goodbyes, Alex waited in the car until Liz was safely inside. Even then he still didn't leave. Not like they need him as extra surveillance he mused as he remembered installing more bugs and hiding the camera's in more secured locations. *What are you up to woman?* He started the car and drove back to the office, picking up some fast food on the way and internally groaned at the thought of spending hours spying on her. He had better things to do, like doing the new intern that kept flirting with him. Instead, his orders had been given.

As he sat watching the six monitors that showed every room at different angles, he bit into the greasy burger and sniggered, as he thought back to when they had first brought Liz in for questioning. How innocent and naïve she was back then. And now it appeared she could be related to someone high up on M16's Most Wanted list. Throwing his unfinished burger aside, he leaned forward and sat glued to the monitor that showed her bathroom. He groaned and rubbed himself as he watched her strip off and walk into the glass shower. He continued with his hand job until the glass got too fogged up to see her smooth, soap covered body, and he finished himself off imagining him in the shower with her and how he would fuck her raw.

CHAPTER FOUR

Baited

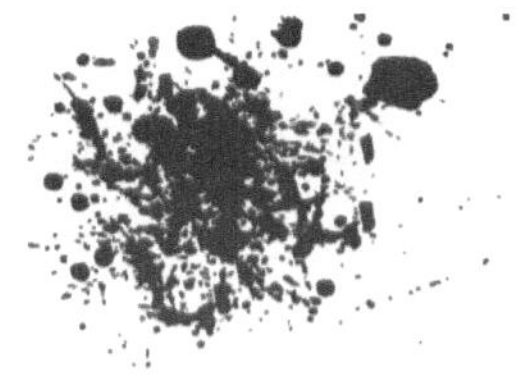

Liz wasn't stupid. She knew she was being kept away from the important stuff and for the last week had been given menial jobs such as filing and research, not what her talents and skills deserved. She made sure Alex and Hart knew how she felt. Liz was ready to walk. Why work for people who didn't trust her? Where did the mistrust suddenly come from?

While she was sitting down proofreading some documents, Alex walked over and told her she was required to sit in a meeting that afternoon. Liz wondered what was so special about that meeting as she had been shunned from all the others that had been held that week.

All she'd learnt was the date and the places the Greek Prime Minister was supposed to visit and the security measures they had put in place.

The hands of the clock seemed to take forever to move

when finally, it was five minutes to two. She eagerly made her way to the conference room. Liz took a seat and waited for the rest of them to arrive.

"Okay," Hart began. "Everything is tightened up and I'm happy and so are the Greeks with the security arrangements we have in place. However, we will be short of surveillance for the banquet that Mr Soulanis will be attending. That's why I've called in an extra team to make sure everything runs smoothly. Miss Finely, you'll be undercover with a team run by Alex."

Liz nodded and then turned her sight to Alex, but his attention was fixed on Hart. She listened carefully to what her role would be and how she should behave and what needed to be done if there was an attempt on the Prime minister's life.

After the meeting ended. Alex told Liz that she would need to practice her martial arts and admitted he was worried that she lacked the skills needed should a situation occur.

∗∗∗

The Prime Minister's visit had gone on without any hitches and so it was now obvious that if the plot wasn't a hoax, then the attack would happen at the banquet. Everyone was on edge, apart from the guests and other dignitaries that knew nothing about the assassination plot.

The dinner and dance had been arranged on the last evening before the Prime Minister was due to leave the UK.

Liz looked in her mirror at the mauve silk gown she wore, she twirled once more before she heard the horn a car. Grabbing a handbag and coat, she rushed out of the apartment and sat in the back of the car. The driver greeted her and then drove to the banquet hall.

***

"Alex, you know you said I should always go with my gut instinct,"

"Mumm," he mumbled as he snuggled into her neck.

They were dancing to a slow waltz. One hand was on her waist, his other held her hand.

"I think something is about to go down."

That captured his attention. He stopped dancing and stared at her before she pulled his hand and led him back into the dance.

"There are too many people stationed around the hall," she explained, "and they are not ours. Two at ten o'clock, standing to the left of the white statue, another on the stairs and then six o'clock, female dressed in the yellow and gold gown, talking to the bloke in grey. The waiters look like they are doing more waiting than serving."

Alex spun her around so he could assess the situation.

"Fuck! You're right, Liz" he whispered. "Shit, why didn't I notice them?"

She thought she knew why. *It's because all his attention has been on me.*

"They've only just moved into position," she said, in the hope that Alex wouldn't be too hard on himself. She had no idea that she was his mission, and his orders were to keep her happy and watch every move she made.

"This place needs locking up tight," he replied and then released her and walked briskly across the dance floor.

Liz turned and walked away in the opposite direction.

Brushing past one of their agents, she whispered, "Lock up." Then moved swiftly away before taking a glass of champagne from a waiter's tray. She walked towards a suited man who was standing talking with a man and woman. She gently tapped him on the shoulder.

"I'm sorry," she apologised to the couple before facing Jones, "Is Smith here?" she asked him and waited a few seconds while the stupid man digested the code word for trouble.

"I thought I saw him over by the bar," he answered. Then he went back to talking to the couple as if nothing was wrong.

Liz swiftly made it to the bar and started talking to Alex while holding her glass of champagne. They small talked, slipping in coded words. And then she caressed his face and kissed him lightly on the cheek before walking towards the ladies' toilets situated on the ground floor.

The corridor was clear, and the back exit was already locked tight. Alex had already sealed the building. By now, Hart would no doubt have secured the Prime Minister and dignitaries inside the banquet hall, as had been arranged. Everyone else was unaware of what was about to go down.

Her job was to take out as many suspected terrorists as she could, preferably without any public casualties.

Doubts started flying in her head. What if she was wrong and caused all this trouble for nothing? But there was no time to waste. She had to be sure. For now, they had the upper hand and needed to secure the suspects before a siege happened.

One of the waiters she suspected was standing alone

outside the kitchen door holding a silver dish of Hors d'oeuvres. Liz walked up to him, smiled, and reached for a canapé.

"What do we have here?" she asked.

"Smoked salmon with cream cheese," he explained with a Greek accent.

Her doubts faded quickly. *Why would there be Greek caterers at an English banquet hall? Okay, the guest of honour was the Greek Prime Minister. Still, why would the catering staff be Greek?*

"Do you have any of those delicious prawn vol au vents?"

"I'm not sure madam."

"Could you be a darling and check for me?" she smiled seductively.

"Okay." He turned and walked into the kitchen.

Liz watched a moment and then followed him through the door. Once inside she slid off to the side, lifted the slit of her dress and took the Glock from her leg holster. With two hands tightly on the gun, she sidestepped and stood up looking straight ahead. There were four workers, three waiters and then the main chef in the kitchen at that time.

Raising her gun, she shouted, "Don't any of you move. Stand where I can see you. Keep your hands high."

They all complied with her orders.

"What's going on? Who are you?" The chef asked in distinct English.

Her eyes went from the workers to the waiters. "There's been a security breach. Stay calm and do what I say."

Before she had time to order them over against the wall, one of the waiters yelled in Greek into a red carnation he wore on his lapel.

"Έχουμε παραβιαστεί."
(We've been compromised.)

Liz pulled the trigger the moment he moved his jacket aside and revealed the black butt of his gun. The bullet hit his chest then he fell to the floor. Gunfire coming from the main hall covered the sound of the gunfire in the kitchen.

A bullet just missed her head as she dived to the left on seeing another carnation wearing terrorist opening fire. Liz saw the chef and the workers on the ground with their hands on their heads, not a position a terrorist would take. So, she knew that it was the waiters that needed to be put down.

Lifting her head, she peered over the top of the metal counter and saw one of the gunmen crouched down behind another silver worktop. Liz couldn't get a clear shot so started creeping closer but needed a distraction. She aimed her gun at the copper pots that hung above the left of his head. The sound ricocheted around the walls giving her enough time to roll out, rest on her left knee, holding the gun out as she took the kill shot.

The gunfire continued outside, as well as inside the kitchen as she covered her head with her hands while the bullets sprayed around her. Squeezing her eyes, she took a deep breath before jumping over the last counter and squeezing the trigger until the last gunman was flat on the floor, unmoving, eyes staring at the ceiling.

Liz ran over to the others who were still on the floor shaking, thankfully not injured by ricocheting bullets. She padded them down for weapons and wires. When she was certain that they were no threat, she told them to leave by the other door and lock themselves in the storeroom.

Carefully, opening the kitchen door, making sure it didn't squeak, Liz crouched down and crawled over to the other side and peered down at the main dance floor. Hostages were in the middle, kneeling with their hands clasped behind their neck, while surrounded by gunmen. Her stomach dropped as she noticed Alex and most of her team among the hostages. Four bodies lay on the marble staircase as their blood flowed down the steps. Another three were dead on the dance floor. She felt sick when she recognised Hart being one of them.

She quietly crawled back into the kitchen and leaned against the cold silver fridge freezer, while her heart was beating out of her chest. She felt physically sick and dizzy. *I'm no hero. There's no way I can consider trying to go up against them. I'm outnumbered, and I'm no fool. I'm fucked!*

Her gun fell to the floor, as she bent her head, and her breathing became erratic. Sweat dripped down her face, her body shook, and her eyes stung as her makeup mixed with her tears. She knew she had to pull it together, get the hell out of there and find help. If any of the terrorists were to come into the kitchen and see the carnage, she knew they would start hunting for her. For now, she assumed they thought they'd rounded all the MI5 agents and security.

Liz had the plan of the building already memorised. The exit she knew was locked up tight. The whole building would have been if her team had done their job correctly. She had to assume that the authorities now knew about the hostage situation. The gunfire at least would have alerted them. Liz needed to find a phone and fast. Leaving the kitchen, she crawled low beside the wall, praying that she wouldn't be seen. Liz could hear the cries and mumbles from down below. *At least the gunfire had stopped.* She continued to crawl to the end of the corridor and then came to another door. She held her breath as she pushed the door open a crack and let out a sigh when she realised it was a staff room. Seeing a telephone mounted on the far left of the wall, she stood up and dodged the chairs and table. Before picking up the receiver, she worried that they might have the phones bugged. But it was a chance she had to take. Calling an untraceable number, she gave them her code, and when connected to whoever was now in charge over there, she told them the situation. She learnt that the building was surrounded. No demands had been made, which she and her superior thought was strange. No one claimed responsibility for the attack. By now someone would have been in touch with the negotiators, but no one had picked up the ringing phone, so negotiations could be made. So, it wasn't clear what the terrorists wanted, who they were, and how they thought they'd be getting out of the building alive.

Her orders were clear. There was no way she was getting out of there and she had to take down as many of the terrorists as she could until special forces stormed in.

At least that was the plan until she heard her name shouted.

***

She recognised that voice anywhere, but what the hell was her father doing here in the middle of a terrorist, hostage takeover? Liz crawled over to the edge of the balcony to make sure she wasn't hearing things. She only saw the back of the man who was cradling an AK rifle in his arms. He was wearing a black dinner suit and had short dark brown, almost black hair. It could have been anyone, but there was no mistaking the man's voice, especially when he called out her name again.

"Ελισάβετ. Finley. If you do not come forward and show yourself, a hostage will be killed every minute you delay, and this will be on your head."

(Elizabeth)

Her heart was slamming in her chest. *Oh my God, my father is the leader of the terrorist group. How, why?* She just couldn't get her head around this and now he wanted her. *What for? I worked for the UK government. I'm an enemy. Is it because I took his men out? Was he going to shoot me? Then it occurred to her that it could have been her father that put the hit on her. But why?*

Elizabeth." He changed back to her English sounding name. "Time is running out, Elizabeth. Bring the hostage here," he demanded.

She watched them drag a woman who was screaming so loud that the one holding her covered her mouth with his hand as he dragged her towards Liz's father.

Liz honestly didn't know what was going to happen next, how it was going to plan out, but one thing was for sure, there was no way another innocent was going to die on her watch, not if she had anything to do with it. She stood up with shaky legs and gripped onto the wooden bannister. Her pulse was running so fast, she felt lightheaded.

"Wait," she called out, as she heard the gun being cocked. "I'm here. Let her go."

All eyes were on her as she slowly walked down the stairs

and into the bloody carnage that used to be the ballroom.

"I'm here, Dad. What is this all about? Why are you doing this?" Liz wanted to cry, but she knew she had to stay strong.

"My love, my child. They have fed you lies. They have trained you to hate the wrong people."

"What are you talking about? I don't understand any of this. Why are you here? Why have you killed these people? Who the fuck are you?"

Without warning her father stepped forward and struck her across the face.

"I won't allow disrespect from anyone, especially family." He spat.

Her cheek blazed where he had hit her. Her jaw felt heavy; she knew it was swollen. A film of tears sprang but she refused to allow one to fall. She couldn't believe he would do that. Who was this man? Her fingers trembled. She didn't know if it was a reaction to her father's hit or shock. Maybe she should have given it a thought before opening her mouth, but then he too never gave it a thought before striking her. One thing she was certain about. Her fear was gone, and now it was the pure wave of anger that swept down her body. She felt her body go rigid as thoughts traversed her mind.

"Respect? You expect respect from me? You're a fucking terrorist, who has just slaughtered innocent people and for what? Huh? What's your noble cause? What are you hoping to gain from this? You'll never get out of here alive; you know that don't you? And as for family! When have we ever been a family? You walked out and left me after Mum died. You have no right to call me your child."

Liz's father grabbed her and before she could do anything, she felt a needle being pushed into her neck and straight away, her breath caught, and she started to cough.

"Elizabeth, listen to me carefully. Come with me, and I will explain everything to you. I will answer all your questions, and I will keep you safe. Please." He held out his hand, but she laughed.

Taking gasping breathes she growled out. "Why the hell would I go" – she held her chest as it grew tighter – "with a murdering bastard. And why would you ever think I would feel safe in your company?"

Liz fell to the floor.

Gasps were heard around the room as her vision blurred. She tried to pull her body up, but she had no strength. Before her breathing stopped, she managed to ask him, why?

"Agree to leave with me now, daughter, or you will die. The injection was peanut oil. Do you agree to come with me? I have the EpiPen and can give it to you now. Hurry, you don't have long left. You are dying, but I have the medicine and I will give it to you if you promise to leave with me."

Her mouth opened trying to take in air.

"Maybe you need more incentive." Her father sneered. "Nico!"

The man named Nico, who was holding the woman hostage, pushed the gun into her stomach, making her scream.

Liz wasn't going to give in to his demands to save her life. But she would if it was to save an innocent.

No longer being able to speak. Liz nodded.

"I'm sorry my love." Her father knelt and jabbed the needle in her neck. She felt the immediate effect as soon as the liquid entered her body. She gasped and gulped in the air her chest needed. And when she could finally speak again, although the words were slurred, she glared at her father.

"Dad, why would you do that? You could have killed me."

Her dad smiled and moved a strand of sweaty hair from her face.

"When I found out you were working for MI5, I knew I had to get rid of you. But I wanted to meet up with you one last time which is why I sent you the coded email. Plus, you gave me plenty of intel, without realizing it. But then after the failed assassination attempt, I received a phone call, and your life suddenly became important to me."

And although she could breathe now, her eyes started to close. She knew that he must have mixed a sedative in with her medicine.

"Take her away and if anything happens to her you will pay with your life."

"How could you do this?" Liz whisper yelled, as she was picked up off the floor. Before sleep took her, she heard her father's last command.

"Kill them. Kill them all"

"No" She screamed over the top of the sporadic gunfire. The screams echoed through her head before a deep sleep took her away.

CHAPTER FIVE

FAMILY HONOUR

When Liz opened her eyes, she quickly closed them again and groaned from the throbbing pain in her head and the impossible vision of her mother sitting beside the bed; the same mother who was supposed to have been killed by MI5, according to her father. But then again, her father was a murdering terrorist.

Not believing she was there, but then just in case it was true, Liz slowly opened her eyes and the same blue eyes, older now, with wrinkles, stared back at her.

"My baby."

"Mum! No, I must be dreaming. You're dead, or am I dead? Maybe the antidote didn't work. What the hell is going on?"

Liz's mother touched her gently on the arm, and that was when she knew that it wasn't a dream. She wasn't dead. Her mother, who was supposedly killed in a car crash, was sitting beside her bed.

"Mum, no." She cried and threw herself at the woman. With her face soaked from tears, she pushed away from her and gently stroked her mother's face.

"How is this possible? You died. Dad said MI5 killed you as you were working as a spy. I don't understand what's going on. Why did you both lie? Why did Dad try to kill me and then kidnap me? What the hell is going on!"

"Oh, Liz, darling, there is so much to tell you. I don't know where to start."

Liz's shock turned to anger

"First, you can tell me why I am talking to my fucking mother who has been dead for over ten years!"

"The crash was staged. I needed to disappear," she said, and bent her head down as though ashamed.

Liz sat back on the bed and stared at her. "But why, Mum. Who are you? And who is Dad working for?"

Her mother stood up and paced the room while Liz waited patiently for the answers.

"Okay, first you're no longer in the UK."

"What the hell!" Liz screamed and jumped off the bed.

"You're in Greece," her mum continued. "Liz, you need to sit down for this."

Liz took a deep breath and did what she was told. Wringing her hands nervously, she waited to hear the truth.

"The reason I had to disappear and the reason you haven't heard from your father is that he is the Boss, the Don of the Greek Mafia. I am his queen, and you are part of this family. His real name is Jacobus Mirisklavou. We have enemies who would try to take the crown, which is why I had to disappear. But I have missed you so much. To keep you safe, we allowed you to live freely for years and kept you away from our lifestyle. But when you joined MI5, we knew it was time for you to return to the family. You are Mafia and now it's time to step up and do what is needed."

To say Liz was gobsmacked was an understatement. She paced the room as her mind went back to the banquet hall. She knew that he was someone in a high position. The guns his men carried and the respect they showed him, should have given it away. *I should have guessed. But the mafia! WOW.* Now there was only one more question she had to ask before she was ready to disown her family and make a run for it.

"Why now? Why am I here? What duty do you expect me to perform for the "family?" She air quoted. "I work for MI5, for Christ's sake. You expect me to start murdering people, go into the slave or drug trade. You're out of your fucking mind!"

Liz was beyond pissed and just glared at the other woman. She was beginning to hate the sight of her mother.

"Your father will speak to you about this. He is waiting for you in his office. And remember, Liz. He's not just your father. He is the King of the Greek Mafia. So, show him some respect."

"King - Queens. You put yourself higher than the royal family." Liz retorted.

Her mother sighed loudly. "My dear, things run differently in mafia families. You will soon learn."

She was about to retort with a mouthful of abuse when the bedroom door opened and two huge men in blue suits stepped into the room.

They bowed their heads down to her mother and then one said, "The Boss has ordered us to fetch Miss Elizabeth." (But they pronounced Liz's name Elisavet, the Greek way.)

"Go," her mum urged.

Her father was the last person she wanted to see or speak to, but as the two guards stepped closer, she knew she didn't have a choice in the matter.

Every step she took down those stairs felt as though she was walking towards her doom. She did not doubt that her dad could kill her without a blink of any eye or remorse. He'd showed his *kind* hand when he almost allowed her to die. She took a deep breath and tried to calm her racing heart. But the closer she got to his office door, the more she had problems breathing. Stepping away from the guards, she held her finger up, motioning for a moment, while she bent her back and held her knees as she tried to stop the panic from rising and waiting for the darkness to recede.

God knows what his men think of me. She didn't want to appear weak so, she stood up straight, took another deep breath and walked straight into the office, slamming the door behind her.

Her dad raised his eyes from his laptop and scowled. He pointed to the chair on the opposite side of his desk.

"Elysavas, κάτσε."

(Sit.)

"My name is Liz, and I do not speak Greek, so if you have something to tell me, talk in the Queen's language," she retorted.

He stood up from his seat. "The only Queen I recognize is my wife, your mother. Now I assume she has told you who I am?"

Liz nodded.

"I don't take disrespect lightly, especially from my mafia family."

Liz stood up. "I may be your daughter, but I am not and will never be part of this mafia."

Before she could react, her father stormed around his desk and his hand came across her face, the force threw her to the floor. She tasted the blood from her busted lip. But even then, she still had more to say.

"You're not even fit for me to call you, my father. You're just a sperm donor and I want nothing more to do with you."

He grabbed her hair and pulled her head, forcing her to stand up.

"You will do as you're told. You've had your freedom and now it's time to do your duty. You are to marry Yuri Ivanhov; he is the son of the leader of the Russian mafia and will take over from his father once you marry. The marriage will create an alliance between our great families, and we will be an unstoppable force."

Again, Liz was speechless, as she let the new information soak in. *I'm betrothed to a Russian mafia underboss, soon to be The Boss who will run the Russian mafia. My father, who has no love for me left me abandoned, and my mother who faked her death, have sold me off like cattle and all for the sake of greed.*

He still had her hair tight in his fist. No matter the pain she turned her head towards him.

"You will never get this alliance as I refuse to marry anyone connected to any mafia."

Her father raised his fist and punched her in the face and then called out for the guards. Before she had a chance to recover or defend herself, she was being dragged out of the office and through a corridor. Her vision blurred from tears, and her head swam as she called out desperately for her mother. Liz heard running of feet and turned to see her mother gasp as she was then pulled down the cellar stairs and into the basement.

She saw empty and full cells as she was dragged past the prisoners who cried out for water and help. Liz felt too weak to react as she was thrown into a cell. Her wrists were pulled up and chained to a damp and cold wall. She hoped her mum would put a stop to this unbelievable cruelty and madness. *I would never treat my child like this.* But as the cell door closed and she waited and waited, Liz knew that there was going to be no reprieve for her and that her mother didn't care that her daughter was incarcerated like some thief or murderer. It wasn't long after they left her chained up, that her head felt too heavy to keep up. Everything ached and she became dizzy and spun into darkness as despair overtook her mind.

When Liz came around, everything hit her at once: the betrayal, the lies, Alex, and every guest including all the dignitaries had been slaughtered, and her parents sold her off like some whore. It was all too much to comprehend, and her mind and body shut down and took her away again. All through the cold and dark days and nights she woke and went under again several times. No one visited her. No food or water was given. Her stomach rumbled and her mouth parched. Her lips became dry and cracked causing the sores to bleed, no matter how much she licked them, it only made them worse. She needed water. Her body weakened until she hung from the chains, unable to stand her weight any longer, unable to even lift her head, even when she finally heard the iron door squeak open and a female gasp.

"Oh, my child," her mother cried. "Why do you have to be so stubborn? Look what you have done to yourself?"

Liz couldn't believe, that even now, she was being blamed for her own incarceration by her so-called parents. *I wish I was adopted.*

"Walk away, woman." Liz croaked and forced her head up to see her mother one last time. "I'm done with you."

Her mother gasped again. "You cannot mean that. Your body and mind are weak. You don't know what you're saying. I'll get you some food right away."

"Why bother?" Liz argued. "Just leave me here to rot and die for, I refuse to be a Russian whore."

"So stubborn," her mother tutted, before turning to leave.

Liz wondered why her mother left the cell door open. Was she going to expect another visitor so soon? Did her mother think that by some miracle she could find the strength and somehow get out of the chains and escape? Liz chuckled at the thought and couldn't even raise her arms to test the strength of the chains.

Not long after, a servant came into the cell and tried to get Liz to eat some soup, but Liz kept her lips tightly shut and refused to eat. She wouldn't put it past her father to drug or put nuts inside. So, she wasn't going to take the risk. She knew her body needed nourishment. She wasn't quite ready to give up yet, but she also wasn't going to play by their rules.

Liz now wished she had taken the food and water offered, and that her father didn't just walk into the cell holding a thin leather whip.

With no strength to fight, she didn't react when two of

his guards, unchained her hand and hooked up her arms up to the ceiling in the middle of the cell. She didn't even try to stop them and couldn't turn to see what was happening as her father and the guards stood behind her.

"You will learn how to respect me." Her father yelled before she heard the slicing of the air as the whip slashed her back.

Liz screamed, as much as her dry throat allowed.

"You will learn your place."

Liz heard the swish again before she felt the pain of the second strike. All she could do was hang there and cry.

"You will embrace your family and do your duty."

Two lashes came down harder and then another. Her body was broken but she still had her spirit and was determined to find a way to escape from the hell she was in. Black spots started to appear in her blurred vision.

"Get her down and take her to the infirmary, make sure she is treated well and that she eats."

***

When Liz woke, she was lying on her stomach. She couldn't move and couldn't see much from where she was. But she knew she was in some sort of hospital. She tried to lift her head before the pain ran through her body and she fell unconscious again. The second time she awoke, she was on her front almost sitting, propped up with pillows. An IV was attached, feeding her, giving her body the food and strength, it needed. She was only alone for a few minutes before her mum came in and rushed to her side, with a face full of concern.

"Oh, darling, my Liz, you're awake, finally. You've been

unconscious for days. I was so worried."

Liz tried to answer her, but her voice just croaked out the word 'water' instead. Her mother held her head and helped her to drink the cool refreshing liquid. Liz thought it tasted amazing.

"How long have I been here?" she asked.

"Five days, darling. You had a fever but it finally broke. Your back is healing nicely. You know, you should never have pushed your father like that. He doesn't want to hurt you. You are his only heir."

Before she had time to retort with a sarcastic comment, the door opened and the last person she ever wanted to see again, walked in.

"Elizabeth, how are you?"

Liz lifted her head and sighed. "I still have some pain, sir."

His eyes lit up on her use of the word sir.

He wants a polite, respected submissive daughter, that's who he will get until I'm fit and able to escape.

"Rest, now. You will be meeting your fiancé next week and I want you strong and beautiful again." He stared at her waiting for her reaction and retort.

"I will do my best to recover quickly, sir."

He nodded and then turned and left. Her mum stood up and leaned over and kissed her on the forehead.

"Good girl. You will quickly learn how to be a good wife and you will eventually fall in love with him." She stood looking down at Liz and fidgeted, as though she wanted to say something else. Then shook the thought away and attempted a smile.

"Let's get that IV out of you and some real food in your

stomach. You've lost a lot of weight and have the appearance of a skeleton and that just will not do."

Liz watched her leave and then turned in the bed, too angry to allow any tears. Her fists clenched as she pictured how she would brutally kill her father.

***

Unfortunately, Liz recovered fast. Her mother made sure she was able to stand and walk around, back straight, head up as a lady should. Liz was still on pain pills and although her back was healed, the mental and physical scars would be with her for the rest of her life.

***

The days flew by until it was time to meet Yuri, her future husband. She knew nothing about the man and the numerous questions she asked her mother went to deaf ears. What her parents didn't know, was Liz wasn't about to accept this marriage proposal. Even so, she did wonder what married life to a Russian mafia leader would be like. Hollywood Housewives? Don't have to break a nail on any housework, just be a whore in his bed, look good by his side in public and sprout out Russian children for him. Or would she be chained to the kitchen sink, forced to do all the housework, never allowed to leave his castle, but again expected to be a whore in bed and a baby-making machine? Whichever way it turned out; it was not the life for her. Liz just wanted to get the meeting over with and find some way to get back to the UK and protection. That is if she was still working for MI5 and not now on their most wanted list!

Her mother made sure she was up at 6 am even though the meeting wasn't until 4 pm that afternoon. She had designers, a makeup artist, and hairdressers all lined up to pamper and make sure Liz appeared beautiful for her fiancé. But Liz felt like she was being prepared for sacrifice. The truth was she was nervous. For the last few days, she had kept her comments and mouth shut, only talking two or three words to answer a question. Mealtime was silent and strained, although her mother tried to get some conversation going with light banter and false smiles.

She was taken to her father's office when her mother was finally happy with Liz's appearance.

Knocking on the door, she waited for her father to shout,

"έλα μέσα." (Come in.)

Liz walked inside and stood by his mahogany desk. Her hands were clasped in front. Her head was down, behaving like the sub he wanted. She stayed silent and unmoving.

"Yuri is a powerful man." Her father's commanding voice echoed around the room. "And once you are married and he becomes the head of the Russian mafia, you will be expected to be an obedient, polished wife. You should think very hard about your performance today. Yes, I'm not stupid, Elizabeth, I know this is all an act to appease me and make sure you're not punished again. But don't think that you can drop this charade. This will be your life. Get used to it. You may now speak."

She lifted her head and stared at the man she hated. "I have nothing left to say to you."

He glared at her hard, before dismissing her with a wave of his hand.

Her mother was waiting outside the office. "How did it go? Is he pleased?"

Liz ignored her and walked into the sitting room, where the meeting with Yuri was supposed to take place.

"Don't think for one moment you can give your husband the same silent treatment. He wouldn't stand for such disrespect." Her mother spat.

The front doorbell rang, and her mother clapped. She ran out of the room, shutting the door, leaving Liz alone with her thoughts and a fast-beating heart.

The door opened and her father walked in first, then her future husband. She paid no attention to her mother as she couldn't remove her eyesight from Yuri. He was a giant and his shadow covered her father. He had dark, almost black eyes. His hair was cut short and cropped on the top. But his muscles shaped the giant's body. She waited until everyone was seated and then sat down. Liz gulped and blinked, then sat up straight as introductions were made. Her mother who was sitting beside her, sat with her head bent down. Not looking at either man in the room. *Is this how I'm expected to behave?* Not wanting to cause any trouble she sat silently, her eyes focusing on her clasped hand on her lap, while the men who were seated together on the opposite couch, chatted wholeheartedly. But the talk was all business and Liz was about to sneak in a yawn when the door opened again and a tea trolly was pushed in. Liz immediately noticed there were only two cups. Her mother and father stood up. Father bowed to Yuri.

"I will leave you two to get to know each other better. We shall speak again in my office before you leave."

"Да, we will."

His voice is rough and dominant, born to be the boss of the Bratva.

Liz waited until they had left the room before turning and looking Yuri in the eye.

"I am sorry you have flown all this way for nothing. But I have no intention of becoming your wife. I have no intention of having anything to do with the mafia: Greek or Russian."

"You were born into this world. You are mafia whether you like it or not. You will be my *zhena*. (wife) No mistake. When I am King, you will be my *Koroleva*. (queen)

Yuri bent down and held her chin up, so she had no choice but to look at him.

"Stand up," he ordered. "You know nothing of my world, but I am willing to train you. You will address me as 'sir' when in public and 'daddy' when in the bedroom."

Liz gasped and took a step back. "I know you think you're a big man, but no man, boss or not, will EVER tell me what to do."

Before she had time to react, his huge hand had grabbed her throat, and he dragged her across the room. Her feet hardly touched the cold tiles of the floor. Her breathing became laboured. *If he squeezes any tighter, he will crush my windpipe.* Her back slammed into the wall. He allowed her feet to touch the floor again, but still not allowing her to take full air.

"Hmm, I see we have a lot of work to do. You need to learn respect, шлюха!"

He called her a whore. Liz remained expressionless; she didn't want him to know she was fluent in many languages, courtesy of MI5. This was the only weapon she had to wean any information she could use to aid in her escape.

She wondered if he knew she worked for an international intelligence agency. Her thoughts were cut off when his other hand squeezed her breast to the point of pain. He groped her from neck to thighs and all she could do was try to take a deep breath. He then let go of her neck and used both hands to assault her body.

"Umm, I wonder how receptive you are to my touch."

"No!" she yelled as he used one hand to hold her arms above her head, pinning her to the wall, while his other hand went up inside her skirt, pushed her knickers aside, and jammed his finger straight inside her. She screamed at the pain as he continued ramming his large finger in and out.

"Umm nice and wet for me." He grinned. "You like this, my whore?"

He rammed another finger inside of her, and her body betrayed her, as she felt her juices run down her leg.

"Stop, please," she begged.

Her stomach was tightening up, but she wasn't going to allow her body to orgasm. She was determined not to give him that gift. He stuck a third finger inside of her as his thumb started rubbing her clitoris. She felt stretched to her limit, as his three fat fingers continued to assault her.

His other hand covered her mouth as she screamed in pain.

"Nice and tight. Just how I like my моих блядей." (Bitches)

He didn't stop ramming his fingers, further into her.

"Yuri, stop, please. It hurts," she cried.

She'd been tortured before, and she just about coped with that, but the sexual punishment wasn't something she'd ever experienced, and she knew then, that if she married that monster, she would be raped and punished every day and night as she would never give herself to him willingly. She felt disgusted with herself for allowing him to assault her and give him the satisfaction, he craved.

"Beg me to." He spat at her and then grabbed her breast and squeezed her nipples, before covering her mouth with his giant hand again as she screamed at him to stop. She didn't know how much more punishment her body could take. He removed his hand so he could hear her beg.

"Please, sir, please stop. No more." Liz felt she had degraded herself by doing as he ordered.

"Call me, daddy." He smirked.

"Okay, okay," she screamed out. "Daddy, please, stop."

He smirked and removed his fingers before stepping away and licking her juices off his hand.

"Delicious! You will make a good submissive. I am satisfied."

Even with the cramp and the pain down below, she stood up straight, spat in his face and punched him as hard as she could. Anger for what she allowed to happen made her fight back and prove to herself and him that she would not be taken that way again.

"Don't you ever put your hands on me. No matter what my father has told you, I am no sub; I would rather die than become your sex slave."

"Bitch," he yelled, before punching her in the stomach.

"You will learn to respect your master." His boot kicked her stomach as she laid helpless on the floor. "You will be an obedient wife." He kicked again.

Liz crawled into a fetal position holding her stomach as

tears ran down her, forming a puddle on the cold tiles she laid on.

He crouched down so she could hear him. "The next time we meet, my Queen, you will be taking my fist, so get used to the pain. There will be rules, and you will be punished if you break any of them. For now, you will address me as 'sir' and speak only when told to." Yuri stood up just as the door opened.

"I hope you find her to your liking?"

"She needs to work on her manners. I assume you will take care of that?" Yuri said.

"She will be ready."

"Do not touch the face," Yuri said. "The wedding will take place in Russia, in one month. Will that give you enough time to have her ready to receive me?"

"Да," her father answered. "Yes. She will be compliant."

Liz lay completely still. She closed her eyes as she waited for them to leave. She heard the door shut and thought she was alone until her hair was grabbed and she was being pulled out of the room. Liz screamed and reached up to the hands that pulled with such strength. She knew who it was, and she knew what was going to happen next.

"No, Dad. Please don't! Sorry, Dad," she cried.

"Whore," he yelled back.

"All you had to do was be polite and behave, but no, you had to embarrass me. Well, now you're going to learn what happens when you disrespect me, this family, and my name. I went easy on you before. He wants a submissive wife. I will make sure he gets one. The next time you meet, you'll be licking his shoes.

***

Liz lost count of the days she was beaten and starved until unconscious. Her father kept her weak until he broke her. Her mother nursed her back to health and so it continued until her body didn't know what was happening. Her spirit was slowly breaking, and she couldn't see a way out of the darkness. The bruises and welts from the whips may heal, but she would never forget what her father and his lackeys had done to her. And she would never forgive her mother for standing by and allowing it to happen. *Doesn't she have any self-respect or love for me?*

***

Liz knew the time for being shipped off to Russia was nearing. There was excitement in the air. Her mother had a permanent smile on her face and fussed around her, making sure Liz was comfortable when resting and suitably dressed to meet with her father. Every day she was bought down into his office where she knelt in front of his desk, head lowered and listened to his orders and rules of how she should behave and treat her future husband.

Yes, she would play along with them, let them think she had given up and was ready to do their bidding, when in fact, she had given up! She would be the mindless doll they wanted but there was no way Liz was going to allow herself to be abused and degraded by a monster like Yuri. She had it all planned. The night before she was due to leave, she would take the pills she'd been hoarding and lock herself in the bathroom with a bottle of Vodka (Russian) of course, take the pills and slit her wrists. She would make sure there was no way she would survive. Yes, she had given up. Given up on life. And she was ready to be done with it all. If her life couldn't be on her terms, then she would fucking make sure her death was!

So, she went through the charade of a party with her father's mafia family, to celebrate the oncoming wedding and what he believed would be an alliance between the two mafia families. Yes, she played her part well, knowing she wouldn't have to suffer much longer. She was ready for it all to end.

***

Her mother was in her 'Mother of the Bride' form and gushed about all the different designer wedding dresses Liz was going to be trying on that day at the boutique. She just wanted to throw up at how fake it all was. Her mother knew just as well as she did that it was all a sham. She was putting on a good act in front of the family knowing what life Liz was about to be forced into.

A black SUV dropped them, and two other women, who Liz had no idea who they were and two of her male Greek cousins she'd never met, outside a wedding shop in the centre of the town. The women gushed at the dresses in the window, before her mum pushed Liz through the door.

Liz peered at the men standing either side of her mother and wondered if they were guarding the 'Queen' or making sure she didn't escape. Liz guessed it was the last one at the way the men glared at her. Their expression saying, 'just you try.''

No one asked her opinion on what dress she wanted. This was her mother's show, and Liz being her only daughter, she was making sure to show off her daughter's beauty and the mafia family's wealth. She described the dress she wanted Liz to wear, as though she'd already picked it out of a magazine. At least she was allowed the champagne that was offered to her. She smiled at the lady as she took the last champagne flute from the tray. The lady smiled back, but Liz could tell it was forced, and that made her wonder if she felt pity for her or was jealous. *I'm happy to swap places with you if that's the case.* Liz took a sip before the glass was taken from her, and a pure white silk wedding dress was put over her head. Once the lace at the back was tightened it gave her an hourglass waist, she glanced in the mirror, and someone who represented a marshmallow stared back at her. Liz cringed at her reflection, and the lady who offered her the champagne glass back then bit her lip and looked sad for her.

Liz pointed to a straight lace dress that was hanging on a rail to the left of her. She let her mother have her say in everything. But there was no way she was going to look like a meringue on her wedding day.

What am I thinking? There's not going to be a wedding. At least the bride won't be there. She chuckled to herself as she pictured her parents' reaction when they found her dead. Liz smoothed down the dress and stared at her now silhouette figure. Taking the drink back off the lady, she downed it before having the courage to go out and face her mother's wrath. Then the lady opened the curtains, and Liz walked out to

"Very beautiful. You're a doll. You're a princess."

The rest of the staff and females in the shop praised her beauty, all apart from her mother, who sat with folded arms and a frown on her face.

Liz took the lady's hand, as she helped her to stand on the pedestal while the assistant brought over a lace veil. Liz shook her head to it and then felt woozy. Her vision started blurring and she felt herself falling off the box step but didn't feel the ground as strong arms caught her. She felt herself being carried away. The last thing she heard was an explosion and screams before everything went black.

CHAPTER SIX

A New Reality

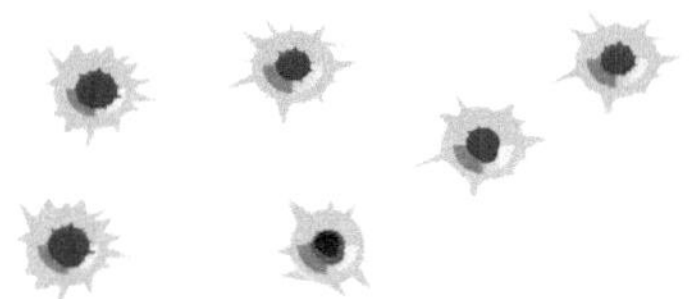

When Liz woke up, she thought she was back to the torture training in the MI5 as she found herself tied to a chair, still wearing the now not so white wedding dress. She had hoped it was all a dream and that she was still being interrogated when she heard the door open and, she watched two largely built suited men walk in. Liz saw one smile and the other scowl, and she knew she was about to live a scary reality.

"Buongiorno Principessa."

(Good morning, Princess.)

Again, she was fluent in Italian but didn't want them to know that. So, she raised her head and said, "Who are you? Where am I?"

"No. We ask the questions. Now tell me where Daddy's warehouses are?"

"I've no idea what you're talking about."

"We will do this the hard way."

Liz watched one of them take a tool, similar to pliers, from a table and walk back over.

"What are you doing? No, please. I'll tell you anything I know. Just don't do this."

"Last chance."

"I know nothing about the work my father does. I didn't even know he was mafia until a month ago. Please, you have to believe me."

The blonde man who held the tool tutted before she watched him rip the nail off her middle finger. Liz screamed and shut her eyes tightly as the stinging pain ran up her hand to her arm. She shook, as the tears soaked her cheeks.

"Why are you doing this?"

She screamed as he pulled off another nail and then another. Liz couldn't catch her breath. Her heart was racing, black spots appeared before she fell into darkness and could no longer feel any pain.

Liz woke again, but this time she found herself hanging from her hands, her toes barely grazing the floor. Shackled to a beam fixed to a low ceiling, she was stripped down to her white lacy underwear, her arms were stretched to the limit, and she felt her body breaking. The pain that came from her hands made her realise she had lost more than a couple of fingernails.

Liz had only been awake for a minute or so before the door opened and another man, again dressed in a suit, came in. He walked straight up to her and smiled as his eyes followed down her body.

"Bellissima."

(Beautiful) "It will be such a shame to ruin this body."

Liz shivered. "Please, I don't know what you want. I told you I don't know anything about what my father did."

"That's hard to believe." He sniggered. "You are the princess of the Greek mafia, heir to the throne and betrothed to Yuri Ivanhov, underboss to the Russian mafia; Two of our biggest rivals."

"Yes, but under duress," she argued.

He laughed. "Principessa (Princess). I don't care about any of that."

He gripped her chin and glared at her. "You are not innocent, so cut the act. I want to know where your father keeps the drugs, money and weapons!" he yelled.

"I don't know." She cried; her face now wet with tears. "We never talked about the mafia. All he cared about was the marriage and the alliance." She silently prayed that she'd given him enough information to let her go and stop the torture.

"Such a shame."

He walked behind her and that's when she heard the leather whip through the air before she felt it slash her back, ripping open her skin. He put full force into each blow, and she screamed and begged him to stop until her throat gave out. She could feel and smell the blood as it dripped down her back and legs. Unable to hold herself up any longer, her body sagged, and her head bent before she lost consciousness.

The torture continued for days. As well as being left hanging in a cell that stunk from her waste, she was cut, whipped, starved, but she had nothing to tell him. It was the same man who wouldn't stop the torture. He rubbed salt into the open cuts and squeezed lemon juice onto her back. Never had she felt so much pain and she knew she couldn't take much more. Her body was too weak, they were slowly killing her. She realised that the so-called torture she got from the MI5 setup was playtime compared to what the Italians had done to her.

She woke again as a bucket of cold water was thrown at her. With blurred vision and not being able to speak clearly, she croaked out as loud as she could.

"Voglio parlare con il tuo Capo."

(I want to speak to your boss.)

She saw his surprised face before her head fell forward and darkness hit her again.

A violent slap on her cheek caused her eyes to snap open. No longer hanging from the ceiling, she was now sitting with her hands tied behind a chair. A thin blanket had been wrapped around her shoulder hiding the state of her body. It took a moment for her vision to clear. Then she heard a clear voice call out in Italian ordering someone to give her water. The tone of his voice sent shivers through her, and her stomach fluttered. She knew she'd never heard the man before. A cup was raised to her mouth, and she greedily gulped the water down until she started to choke and splutter.

The cup was removed, and the man that had spoken previously walked up to her and crouched down so she could see him.

"Do you know who I am?"

Liz stared at the Italian god. He was gorgeous, with high sculptured cheekbones, tan skin, and the bluest eyes she'd ever seen, His black hair was short, but still long enough for him to tug at, which is what he was doing as he waited for her response.

Yes, she knew exactly who he was, although they'd never met, he had been part of her homework, courtesy of MI5. She stayed silent and shook her head.

"My name is Marco Lucianno, and I am the Don. The Boss of the Italian Mafia."

Her mouth feigned shock. Now she knew she was in deep shit and why they were trying to get information out of her.

"Principessa." He said as he stroked her cheek with the back of his hand, causing her to shiver but not in fear. "I don't want to hurt you. You have been through enough, so tell me the whereabouts of your father's warehouse and docks."

Liz watched his expression hoping he would see her sincerity.

"Please, I don't know the answers to your questions. Believe me. I would have told you by now than go through all that torture. If I knew anything, I would tell you. I have no love for my father."

Marco's eyebrows raised.

Now that I have his attention, I can only hope he will believe me. Leaving out that she worked for MI5, she told him about her father kidnapping her in the UK. She told him the lies that had been fed to her, about the arranged marriage and what her father and Yuri did to her. Liz cried out her truth.

"Please, believe me, Mr Lucianno. Let me go or kill me now as I can't take any more of these cruel beatings. I am innocent. If I knew anything, I would gladly tell you. I beg of you, don't hurt me anymore. Just let me die, as I have nothing to live for anyway."

Marco's face held no expression. She watched him and the other man walk out of her prison. The door slammed shut, and she was left alone as she cried in pain and wished for death.

***

Liz knew before she opened her eyes, she was no longer in her cell. There was no odour of rotten flesh and piss and faeces. She was no longer sitting on a hard, wooden chair but was laying on the soft bed. Opening her eyes, she stared at a cream ceiling with intricate plastered designs. With no strength to even sit, she turned her head and saw an IV attached to her left arm. Her eyes searched around the room; she was alone. But before she could admire the rest of the room, exhaustion took her. Her eyes closed and she slept.

Murmurs from two people close by woke her, but she didn't want to open her eyes and so stayed still as she listened to their conversation. She soon realised a male was talking to a female doctor and asking about her condition.

"When will she wake? It's been days."

"You need to be patient. Her body is weak and has been through much. She needs rest and will wake when she's ready."

Before they left, the doctor said. "I hope what you did to this poor lady was worth it?"

The man never answered, and Liz waited until the door closed before relaxing. No matter what happened next, for now, she was warm, pain-free, comfortable, and feeling unexplainably safe.

***

Liz woke to the aroma of strong coffee and baked pastries. A lady wearing a black dress with a white pinafore, smiled at her, as she carefully placed the breakfast tray on the bedside cabinet.

"Buongiorno signorina."

(Good morning, Miss.) The maid greeted.

Liz wasn't sure if she should give away that she knew Italian, so, for now, she just smiled and attempted to sit up, but then grimaced and squeezed her eyes closed from the pain of where the whip had sliced through her back. The maid gently helped raise her and made sure the pillows were supporting Liz's back. She then took two white pills off the tray and gave them to Liz along with a glass of cooled water. Liz swallowed the pills and guzzled down the refreshing water, and then the breakfast tray was carefully placed on Liz's lap before the maid pointed to the camera in the corner of the room.

Liz didn't feel like she was shown it as a warning, but more like if you need anything, let us know, we are watching. Liz gestured her thumb up at the camera, before smiling back at the maid. Liz felt uncomfortable having the maid feed her, but her hands were bandaged stumps. But she knew she still had her fingers, as she could feel a sting every time she tried to move them. The sweet cakes and the biscuits were obviously homemade, and she savoured every crumb. The coffee was strong but smooth. She never had Italian coffee, but she liked it.

The rest of the day was spent sleeping, awake and worrying where the hell she was, what was going to happen to her, and being fed delicious snacks and hot dishes the was brought in many times during the day and evening.

The following morning, she was gently woken by the same maid that had been serving her. Helping Liz out of bed, she walked her to the bathroom, where a bath of lavender and floral petals awaited.

The maid carefully covered Liz's bandaged hands in plastic bags before helping her sit in the warm bath. Liz was careful as she laid back, but it was as though the bath contained some sort of oil or treatment as her back became numb and painless. Liz closed her eyes and laid there for a while before the maid started to wash the blood and grime of Liz's body, again feeling helpless as she couldn't do it herself.

Tears started falling and she couldn't brush them away. The maid gently wiped her cheeks with a sponge and squeezed her shoulder, just to let her know that she cared and understood. So much was said between them without words.

But Liz couldn't stand the silence and so turned her head and spoke.

"Come ti chiami?"

(What is your name?)

"Maria." The woman answered with a beaming smile.

"I am Elizabeth. Thank you for all your help."

After the bath, Maria took the dressings off Liz's hands and fingers and gently put ointment where the nails should have been. Maria told her that they would soon grow back, patting the back of her hand gently. Liz watched and was surprised by how painless the treatment was. After they were wrapped up again, Maria put cream on Liz's bruised and battered face and then redressed Liz's wounded back. The touches and mothering compassion Maria was showing made her think of her own mother. Her mother was so different from Maria, so cruel. Liz sobbed again and Maria gently hugged her until Liz stopped crying. She didn't want to see the damage to her body. She knew she'd be scarred for life. She didn't want to know how long she'd been tortured for or how long she'd been in recovery. After the she stopped crying and the treatment was completed, Liz felt stronger in her mind and body. Her spirit felt stronger, and she was able to walk with her back straight and without Maria's aid as she entered the bedroom again.

"The doctor will be visiting again soon. Rest now."

Liz nodded and then laid back in bed, relaxed, and soon fell back to sleep.

Another three days passed before she finally got permission from the doctor, to be allowed to walk around and that was after she could prove she could balance on one foot and stand with her back straight, which was harder than it sounded. Liz knew her skin had either been stitched together or stuck with glue, as every stretch caused a twinge in her back, shooting a wave of pain down her centre. It was with supreme effort that she kept her face clear and did not grimace.

Until she knew what was to be her fate, she didn't want to show too many emotions. She was comfortable with Maria, but the idea of dealing with the others made her feel vulnerable.

In all the days she'd spent in the room, she'd never seen Marco or any of his men. *It's not like he should care about my health, the damage he caused. I'm a prisoner after all.*

Maria was there the next morning and told her that the Boss wanted to see her in his office. She helped Liz dress and make her presentable to meet the Don. Maria changed the bandages on her hand. Each swollen finger was carefully treated, and only small dressings covered the tips. Liz sighed as she wiggled them a little. She was free to use her hands again as long as she was careful. Finally, she could feed herself.

Liz's stomach was rolling, and she couldn't eat anything for breakfast. She just wanted to get the meeting over with and see where she stood. Her life was in his hands.

The stairs weren't too wide, the problem was the number of them. The Boss's office happened to be on the ground floor of the mansion she was walking around. And as luck would have it, or not, there were no lifts. *How do the maids manage to walk up and down these stairs all day?*

Now standing outside a mahogany door, she wiped her sweaty hands on the dark blue tea dress she was wearing. Tucking a strand of her brown hair behind her ear, she lifted her fist to knock, when his voice rang out loud and clear.

"Entra."

(Come in)

Liz walked inside, keeping her head low as a sign of respect. She stood in front of his desk and then greeted him, in his language.

"Buongiorno."

(Good morning.)

He gestured to a seat. "Sit."

They stared at each other until Marco lowered his eyes down at an open file in front of him.

"We will talk in English, so there is no loss of translation, although, from what I've heard, you speak excellent Italian. But then being trained by MI5, I assume you are fluent in many languages." He raised his eyebrows and waited.

"Seven," Liz answered his silent question.

"Hmm, good," Marco answered, as he rubbed his chin. "I do not forgive easily. I do not do charity and if what you had told me didn't check out, you would be ten feet under by now."

Liz swallowed.

"I will not apologize for the treatment of you. The same would happen to any enemy whom I capture. However, it seems we both have the same enemies now." He was staring at her waiting to hear her speak.

"The Greek and the Russian mafia."

"Indeed."

Liz adjusted herself on the chair. "Tell me. What happens now? Am I still your prisoner? What is my worth to you when I know nothing that can help you destroy my father or Yuri Ivanhov?"

Marco walked around the desk and stood in front of Liz. "Stand up!" He ordered. She did what he said.

"You are now the property of the Italian mafia. Be thankful you have enough skills to be useful to me." He took a step back and looked her up and down. "You belong to me now and will follow any order I give. Do you understand?"

Liz breathed deeply and holding her head up she said. "Yes, Don. I understand."

Marco smiled and walked back around the desk.

"Good. You will come to dinner tonight and I will introduce the family to you. Your new family. You will show respect and honour, and when you have proven yourself, they will return that love and respect. You will be expected to attend breakfast at 8 am. Lunch you can organise for yourself, but we all have dinner together at 7 pm. Never be late and make sure you dress accordingly. Your room has whatever you need, and Maria will be available to you, should you require assistance or anything. You may walk around the house, but I wouldn't advise it unaided, as there are guards and my men walking and out all day and not everyone will know who you are, and I will not be held accountable if something happens to you. Do I make myself clear?"

"Yes, Don. I am basically to stay in that room until I'm needed or called for."

Marco sighed. "I never said that. Listen closely because I don't like to repeat myself. You may walk around the house, but you are not allowed outside these walls unaccompanied and certainly not off the ground. When you are fit and able, you'll start your training. I want to see what the UK government has taught you. Take this weekend to rest and socialize. Do you have anything you want to say?"

"I understand I am mafia now, even though I refused this from my own family. I know I have no choice and I will have to prove myself to you. As to belonging to you, I am no whore and any man, mafia or not that tries to force themselves on me, I won't hesitate to kill."

Marco rushed around the table grabbed hold of Liz's hair, pulling her off the chair and pushed her onto his desk.

"Don't ever talk to me like that again, girl! Do you

understand? I will make sure my men know you are not to be touched. But don't ever think you are free. You do belong to me, Elizabeth. You will address me as Don or Boss when in company and Marco when we are alone. I hold your life and can extinguish it out any time I want. Prove to me I have not made a mistake in keeping you alive."

Marco's pressed his body against hers to force her spine to arch backwards. A shooting pain ran through her, causing her to move toward him. Liz shivered as his eyes raked her body, lingering on her breasts. To her horror, her nipples hardened, eager for his touch. She felt his breathing become uneven and his hardness brush against her lower belly. A trickle of wetness down her thighs along with dull throbbing brought a different kind of pain. Her eyes fluttered to his, heat shimmered in them but just for a second. He blinked away whatever he was feeling, grabbed her arm and pulled her away from him until they were standing apart but close.

"Now leave. I have work to do." His voice sounded huskier than before. Liz squeezed her thighs to ease the ache in her. Her subtle movement didn't go unnoticed by Marco, and he smirked before dismissing her from his thoughts and his office. Liz returned to her room and laid on the bed as she tried to figure out what he had said and what she had just agreed to. *Holy shit! I'm the heir to the Greek mafia, betrothed to the Russian mafia and now belong to the Italian mafia. Fuck! He's gonna make me sign and swear the Omerta. If I don't, he will kill me and if I do, I lose my freedom. How the hell did I get into this mess?*

CHAPTER SEVEN

OMERTA

Liz was dreading meeting the "family" as he called them and certainly had no appetite. Her nerves were messed up and it wasn't until Maria came into the room to help her dress, that she realised she had stayed in bed staring at the wall for hours. She had no idea it was so late. Her stomach churned.

"May I give you some advice?" Maria said softly in Italian. Liz nodded.

"Don't speak unless they ask a question. Don't look them in the eye. Keep your head down, eat quietly and be respectful. They don't know you. They won't trust you and you need to earn their respect, but they will expect respect from you right away."

"Grazie. Capisco."

(Thank you. I understand)

Maria picked out a red knee-length skater dress. It was modest and covered her arms. Liz still has fading bruises on her face and her fingers were still sore and swollen. She had difficulty holding a hairbrush and her hands didn't have the strength to get the tangles out of her hair, so

Maria combed her hair and put it half up and half down, then curled the tips. Mascara and a little lip gloss finished off her look. Wearing flat silver shoes, she followed Maria downstairs and then stopped outside the office door.

"The Boss wants to speak with you before dinner."

Maria touched Liz's arm. "Good luck."

"Grazie," Liz answered, and took a deep breath before knocking on the door.

"Entra," Marco called out.

Liz walked inside the office, with her head down and stood beside his desk.

"Please sit," he said. "You may look up. Before we go to dinner there is one small matter we need to address. I'm sure you know what the Omertà is?"

Liz swallowed before answering. "It's a code of silence."

Marco nodded. "That is correct. Do you know what will happen if you break the Omertà?"

"I and anyone I have talked to about your business will be killed."

Marco slid a piece of paper over to her and gave her his fountain pen. "Good, then sign and we can go to dinner."

Her hands shook as she took the pen, knowing if she signed, she was giving her oath and life to the Italian mafia. Then again, if she refused to sign, Marco would probably pull out his gun and shoot her where she stood.

Taking a deep breath, she signed on the dotted line above Marco's signature.

He smiled and took the paper and put it in the top drawer of his desk. "Now that this is out of the way, let's eat."

Liz turned, and it was the first time she'd seen him smile. He held his arm out and she took it. Holding on to his arm lightly, they walked out of the office and into the dining room.

Liz nearly stopped walking when she saw how many people were seated around the long table. The chatter stopped and all eyes turned to them.

Everyone stood up and waited for Marco to sit at the head of the table.

Liz stood still, head, bent, low, not knowing where to sit.

There was movement around the table and then Marco called out to her.

"Elisabetta, come sit." He pointed to a now-empty seat beside him. Liz kept her head down as she walked, making sure not to glance at any of the other people at the table.

"Grazie, Don."

(Thank you, Boss.)

Once Liz took her seat, talk around the table continued. She listened to the different conversations as she nibbled on each course that was placed in front of her. No mafia business was discussed, and she assumed it was because they didn't trust her.

"Why are you not eating?" Marco asked.

She lifted her head. "First, I'm finding it difficult to hold my knife and fork and second. It's been a while since I've had an appetite for food."

Marco huffed, knowing it was a dig at the torture she'd gone through.

"I have the finest chefs in Italy cooking for me and you will not sit and waste food, so eat!"

Liz glanced down at her plate of spaghetti, she wasn't used to such rich tasting food, her stomach was churning.

"Enzo," Marco called out. "When is the shipment coming in?"

Having Liz sitting next to him showed he respected her. Now speaking mafia business in front of her showed the family that he trusted her.

"Thursday evening. Matteo will be picking it up at the docks," the man named Enzo replied.

"Yes, Boss. It's all under control."

Marco nodded, then hit his glass with his knife. "Silenzio."

Everyone stopped eating and the cutlery was put down. All attention was fixed on Marco.

"I think it is time for you to meet our newest edition to the family. Introduce yourself to Elizabetta and if you can, speak in English, although she's fluent in seven languages including Italian.

"Ciao Elisabetta. My name is Enzo, and I am the underboss. This is my wife, Mia."

It was the first time Liz glanced at any of the other diners. Mia was smiling and so Liz tried to smile back, wanting to come across as approachable even though her knees were shaking under the table.

"Ciao." She answered in greeting before feeling a hand on the top of her knee, stopping her leg from shaking. She turned to Marco, and he bent down and whispered in her ear.

"Calm yourself. No one will hurt you here. No one would dare."

"I'm Amera, Marco's eldest sister."

Liz looked at the long, brown-haired beauty. She certainly resembled Marco.

The introductions continued. She met his youngest sister, Gabriella, but was asked to call her Gabby. Liz guessed her age to be around fourteen. She met the Capos: Luca, Mario, Matteo, and Stefano. All were Marco's cousins. Only Luca was married, her name was Elena and Liz didn't get a good vibe from her. Sofia was Mario's fiancé and was in the process of planning the wedding, and bashfully asked if Liz would help her plan. Liz said she would love to if the Don agreed first. Liz was surprised to be asked. Several other names were thrown as her, but it was hard to remember names, but she knew how high they ranked. They were approaching the last two people sat opposite her. A middle-aged lady, who seemed to put her nose up to Liz and the man sitting opposite and next to Marco's left. She recognised him immediately and her body shivered as she remembered the pain he caused her.

He scowled at her before saying,

"Why are we playing nice with this Greek whore? Why is she permitted to sit with the family?"

"That's enough, Nicolo," Marco growled.

"I haven't even started with the princess." Nicolo spat.

Marco leaned closer to her. "You have to forgive my brother. He has no good history with your Greek family."

"Neither do I," Liz mumbled, but it was heard by those close.

Liz turned to face Marco. "May I be excused, Don? I have lost my appetite and don't feel very well."

"Leave, I will send Maria up with some dessert later." Marco said and waved his hands shooing her away.

Liz stood up from her seat. Her eyes were blurry from unshed tears.

"Gracia, buona note."

(Thank you, Goodnight.)

As she walked away from the table, she heard what could only be the spiteful voice of Nicolo's wife.

"Isn't she a spy for MI5? What on Earth possessed you to invite her into the family?"

A loud bang on the table made Liz jump and tears start flowing. Her nerves were shot.

As she left the room, she heard Marco shouting.

"Enough! You forget your place, Sara. You dare to disrespect me. Brother, you teach your whore of a wife, respect, otherwise, I will shut her mouth permanently. And the feud you have with the Greek Mafia will stay in the past. Liz knew nothing of her heritage and is not to be blamed for them taking your suppliers and hurting our business."

Marco stood up from his seat, glared at everyone and then left the dining room. He saw Liz on the stairs.

"Elizabeth, are you okay?"

She turned her head and wiped away the tears.

"Yes, I am fine. Why do you care anyway?"

Marco ran up the stairs and quickly grabbed her arm before she had a chance to run from him.

"Make no mistake, Elizabeth. You belong to me. You are my property, and your wellbeing also belongs to me."

He caressed her cheek with the back of his hand. "Go rest, beautiful." He spoke gently.

Liz just nodded, turned, and continued walking up the stairs to her room.

She tried to sleep, but her mind wouldn't shut off, so she huffed and threw the covers off the bed, pulled on a small, silk dressing gown and slowly opened the door.

The house was silent until the guard standing left of her door asked her if she wanted anything. She jumped and then turned to him. He was a big man, muscled out and had his dark hair styled in a quiff.

"I'm going down to the kitchen to get a drink. Is that okay?" she asked.

"I will accompany you." He said in a tone that told her he was going to follow her anywhere she went.

Liz searched the cupboards for a glass, which the guard was kind enough to get for her. She opened the tap by the sink and waited until the water was ice cold before filling the glass. As she gulped down the cold refreshing drink, she heard someone else come into the kitchen. Turning she saw a tall blonde-haired woman. Liz immediately thought of Barbie, when she looked her up and down and stared at her oversized breasts and plumped lips.

"So, you must be the Greek whore everyone is talking about." She spoke perfect English, but her voice was so shrill. Liz wondered how anyone could put up with her.

"I am the heir to the Greek mafia," Elizabeth answered. "And you must be the fake, plastic slut all the men fuck around here."

Liz felt satisfied at the gob smacked expression on Barbie's face.

"Gino," she screeched. "Are you going to let her speak to me like that? I will tell Marco.

"I wouldn't say anything, Diane. Marco has taken a shine to the Greek princess."

Diana gasped and walked up to Liz and slapped her hard on the cheek.

Gino grabbed hold of Liz's arms before she could retaliate.

"I am Marco's girlfriend and will make sure he hears what you called me, you ugly, disgusting whore." She spat at Liz's feet and then turned and walked away.

"What the fuck!" Liz spat as she struggled in Gino's grip. He didn't let go until Diane had disappeared back up the stairs.

He sighed as he rubbed the back of his neck and suddenly found the floor interesting.

"Gino, is there anywhere I can find something stronger than water around here?"

Gino chuckled. "Yeah, I think you deserve it. Follow me."

They sat together on the couch as she drank the neat whisky, one of the limited editions that Marco collected, and Gino warned her not to touch. While she downed the whisky, he stuck to a soft drink. They both chatted and laughed about tv shows and life in general.

Neither realised how loud their laughter carried until Marco stormed into the room, wearing just his boxers.

"What the hell is going on here!" he yelled.

"Elizabeth met Diane," Gino said, not needing to add any more.

"And you thought it was okay to let her drink half a bottle of my rare, limited-edition whisky? That's 5000 euros a bottle," he shouted at Gino.

Liz spluttered in her glass and then put it back on the table and glanced up sheepishly. "I'm sorry. I just needed a drink after meeting your delightful girlfriend."

"Gino, leave." Marco waited until he'd left before sitting beside Liz.

"She's not my girlfriend."

Liz huffed and shrugged her shoulders.

"What did she say to you to make you so upset?"

"Oh, your fuck partner had a lot to say and a mean right hook," Liz answered and reached for the glass, but Marco took her hand and gently drew circles on the back of her hand, before turning her face and noticing the handprint on her cheek.

"Anyone would think you were jealous, princess."

Liz turned her head and faced him. She could see two heads and she shook her own to try to get her vision back, which was a mistake and made her even more light-headed.

"Look here," she slurred. "I don't need a man. I certainly don't need you. And why the hell would I be jealous of that plastic barbie you've been shagging upstairs?"

He smiled and the butterflies in her stomach started fluttering like they did the first time she heard his voice. *Or could that be the alcohol wanting to come out?*

"Oh, beautiful. You have no idea what you do to me." He moved in closer.

Her head automatically drew closer to his.

"What do you mean?" She whispered as his lips came closer to her own.

"Fuck it, you won't remember this in the morning," he said, before grabbing the back of her neck and pulling her into a passionate kiss.

Both opened their mouths at the same time as their tongues explored each other. The kiss was heated, and Marco had one hand tight around her waist, the other was caressing her breasts. Touching her over the clothes was not enough, he let go of her, allowed his eyes to shimmer down her body, undid the belt of her robe before pulling it off her shoulders. Now all of her was visible to his eyes, and the heat grew in them until it became an inferno that she couldn't turn away from.

"Beautiful," he exclaimed, in a shaken breath, kissing her again and running his fingers down her body to her thighs.

Whether it was lust or alcohol, she didn't know and didn't care, she allowed him to push open her legs as he stroked her covered core.

She moaned at the feeling and the hunger of wanting him to touch her. Marco, on hearing the delicious noises coming from her mouth, wanted to hear more. Moving her panties to the side he rubbed his finger up and down her wet clit before pushing his fingers inside her. He kissed her neck until he found the spot. He smiled as he heard her gasp and become even wetter when he started sucking on the neck making sure he left his mark for all to see.

Liz started panting and held on to Marco's muscled arms as he pumped more fingers in and out of her vagina. The squelching noises put a smile on Marco's face as he increased the speed and kissed her hard while he waited for her to come undone.

Liz felt the fire spread through her stomach as it tightened and she felt an urge to let go of the tightness and when she did, she shattered in his arms as he continued to finger her and rub her clit, making her orgasm last longer. Her legs were still shaking as she tried to calm her breathing down.

She watched Marco take his fingers that were covered in her cum and lick the juices off.

"Delicious. Taste yourself," he ordered, before moving

his fingers to her lips. She sucked the sweet nectar off his fingers until they were cleaned.

"Come, it is late, and you need to rest."

He pulled her off the couch and tied the belt back around her robe. Holding her steady, knowing her legs were still weak after the intense orgasm he gave her, they slowly climbed the stairs and into her bedroom. He laid her on the bed and covered her with the duvet. Kissing her forehead, he watched her eyes slowly closing and the smile on her face lightened his heart.

"You are mine now, beautiful. I have marked you and I will kill any man that touches you."

"And are you also mine?" Liz whispered, without opening her eyes.

"She will be gone by the morning, and you will not see her again. Sweet dreams my Queen."

Liz was softly snoring and didn't hear the last part. She never heard his declaration that he was going to make her his queen and that she would stand by his side.

CHAPTER EIGHT
GUILT

Liz woke to a banging headache even before she opened her eyes. She hated hangovers but was thankfully it wasn't one of those that made her sick. Turning her head, she saw a glass of water, two pills and a note that said DRINK ME. Liz smiled at the kind gesture and took the pills before stumbling over to the bathroom. Her sight was still blurry, she walked into the shower and then remembered to take off the robe before turning the shower on. It was one of those fancy showers that rained on the top of you like a waterfall and the temperature adjusted by voice control. Liz felt like she was in heaven as she stood there, allowing the water to spray onto her, like a massage on her tired and sore body.

As she was washing her hair, the shampoo stung her sore fingers and she yelled out from the pain and then took a pair of plastic gloves, she was supposed to have worn, and forgot, then once her fingers were protected, she stepped back into the shower and continued washing her hair. Liz tried to remember what had happened that night and at once it came crashing back, the step-by-step slides of what she let him do. She stopped the shower and laid her head against the tiles while cursing out loud and wondering how she was going to face him again. Even the regret didn't stop the tickling feeling down below.

"God dammit!" she cursed.

After wrapping a large white fluffy towel around her, she stepped out of the bathroom and squeaked in surprise when she saw Maria standing there with a silver tray in her hands.

"Excuse me, madam. I didn't mean to scare you. The Boss had excused you from attending breakfast but would like you to be on time and formally dressed for dinner. Oh, and he also told me to tell you it will be nothing like the last dinner. Yes, that's all. Oh, he asked me to bring you this small breakfast and to stay and make sure you eat it all." Maria then looked down at the floor, embarrassed.

"How long have you been standing there?"

"A long time, but don't worry, Miss. I didn't want to disturb your bathing time. But I have to say I've never known someone to take a two-hour shower."

"What? Really, I've been in there for two hours? I'm so sorry. I didn't realize. I suppose the breakfast is cold now?"

"Yes, very cold, as the Don asked to bring fruit, pastries and juice."

"Grazie."

Maria smiled and stood waiting, her eyes searching around the room and not directly at Liz as she sat on the bed and munched on the fruit.

"Where is the Don?"

"Out on business."

"Do you know what time he will return?"

"No, ma'am. Is there anything I can help with?"

"It's silly really. Umm – I don't know if I'm his prisoner, worker, or..."

"I understand. Well, I can tell you prisoners don't get this treatment, not from the Boss. I know you're not to leave the grounds."

Liz stared at her hands. "Sadly, I have nowhere to go. I don't even know where this is. I just need to leave the house, get some air, you know?"

"That will be okay. I'm sure Gino will follow you."

"Hmm," Liz mumbled. "Maria, will you be honest with me?"

"As long as I don't get into trouble, yes. What is your question?"

"Is Gino and the other guard, watching me so I don't try to escape or there for my protection?"

"You have sworn the Omerta. You have no friends or contacts here. So why do you think they are by your side 24/7?"

"Thank you, Maria. I'm finished. I may go for a walk on the grounds in a little while.

"Good. Enjoy your walk, Miss."

Liz laid down and her mind played over the conversation. It's good Marco trusted her. She had nothing to hide and no one to count on, so would it be so bad to work for him or even start up something? The last time she had sex was with Alex.

Liz took an intake of breath. Oh God, she never had time to mourn his death or all those innocent people her father slaughtered when he kidnapped her.

Liz never made it to the grounds. She'd been sitting on

the floor beside the bed crying nonstop as she remembered faces and counted the dead all because of her.

My father killed all the MI5 agents, the Greek Prime Minister and his wife, the dignitaries and all those guests, slaughtered because of me and then the Italians killed my mother, my cousins, and the innocent workers in the wedding boutique. All those deaths because of me. And how many more will there be, when the Russian or the Greeks come to get me?

Her mind broke and she felt suffocated and the only way she would find peace and keep everyone safe was if she wasn't around anymore. There was only one thing left to do. Liz stood up on wobbly legs and staggered to the bathroom. Weak with guilt and grief, she locked the door, took the blade out of her razor and without other thoughts she sliced down from her wrist to the middle of her arm. Her blood poured, painting the sink red and she became weak and didn't have the strength to drag the blade deep down her other wrist.

Her legs gave out and she fell kneeling on the floor, her head bent, her vision failing, as she dragged herself over to the bath and rested her head against the tub. She watched as the blood pooled under her limp hand.

I was going to end my life anyway before leaving for Russia. So, I delayed it a few weeks. It was good to meet Marco, but this isn't the life for me. I'll always be looking over my shoulder. I'll never be safe.

Liz remembered how her life was before she ever got the stupid idea to write a book and met Alex. That's when her life took the wrong road, even though it was thrilling, she had no idea what and who was waiting for her. She remembered how it felt when Marco went down on her, his warm tongue pushing its way into her hole. And the earth-shattering orgasm he gave her. That would be something she would always remember and never forget. She could even hear him screaming out her name as the fucked her hard and fast. Liz smiled, sighed, and then realised that they never had sex, it was just her fantasies giving her a farewell gift. Liz closed her eyes and her head slumped forward, as frantic knocking and yelling of her name continued until someone kicked the door in.

***

Marco held her limp hand in his and stared into her pale face. *Why would she do this? Am I not good enough for her? I thought everything was okay between us.*

His gut told him not to leave the house that day. But he had to get to his official office and get rid of the paperwork that had piled up and then he had a competitor hanging in the warehouse waiting for him to get rid of after he got the information he wanted. Marco didn't normally get blood on his hands. He had others he paid good money to do the job for him. But now and again when they finally get hold of a snake, rat, or someone they'd been searching for a long time and has cost him time and money, then he'd be the one to extract the information out of the prisoner.

Marco got the phone call from Gino as he was about to leave for the warehouse. He just wanted the day to be over so he could return to his queen. It was time to get to know her properly and build a stable relationship with her. He needed an heir, and he was certain Elizabeth would be the perfect mother, submissive but he had an idea that she would be a tiger in the bedroom.

145

Gino told him that Carlos, who manned the security cameras, had been noticing Liz's strange behaviour. *What does he mean strange by behaviour?*

Marco immediately clutched his phone and connected it to the cameras inside the house. He went straight to Liz's room, but he couldn't see her. Marco ordered Carlos to rewind the recording. He watched Liz laying on the floor sobbing and his heart broke at the pitiful sight. *Who has hurt her? Is she ill, in pain? Where is Maria?* When he watched Liz stagger to the bathroom and not return, he told Gino to find Maria and for them both to check on Liz. He had that bad feeling in his gut again. His queen needed him, so the competitor's torture would have to wait.

His driver must have broken every road law as he put his foot down and got Marco back to the house fast. He opened the door and heard shouting and crying, but none of the voices belonged to his angel. He ran up the stairs with Enzo and Luca following. Her bedroom door was open, and he could hear Gino banging on the bathroom door asking her to open it.

His heart raced. *Oh no, God please don't let my vision come true.* Everyone moved out of the way as Marco started banging on the door demanding her to open it. Even his threats and curses didn't work. There was silence on the other side of the door, so he stood back and rammed his shoulder into the door, but it wouldn't budge. Enzo seemed to get the same thought and after a count of three, they both kicked the door down revealing Liz sitting up beside the bathtub, with two pools of thick blood on either side of her.

Marco didn't care who witnessed his fears, as he rocked her limp body in his arms. Enzo and Luca wrapped her wrists tightly with the white bath towels, that were quickly turning red.

"Get her to the infirmary and call everyone."

***

Liz had lost too much blood and once they found out that she had a rare blood group type, all of the family were asked and then tested. Nicolo was the only one with the same blood type as her.

The moment Nicolo refused and said his blood was too good to be inside the Greek whore, Marco and Enzo pulled out their guns and aimed them at his head. No one tried to stop them. No one would dare. Yes, they were brothers, but if Liz didn't get that blood she would die and whether she wanted to live or not, he wasn't about to lose his queen. So, under duress, Nicolo gave his blood to the Greek princess he hated.

The blood saved her life, but her mind had shut down due to all the stress and with her body too weak to heal itself, she fell into a coma.

Enzo took over as Boss, while Marco spent his time by her side praying for her to open her beautiful eyes, to come back to him. Certain members of the family made their feelings known about him spending too much time with her and forgetting about the mafia family and his job as Don.

They even caused him to question himself. *Why am I ignoring my duties as the head of the family? Why am I wasting my time with the daughter of the Greek mafia, an enemy of the family, and an MI5 agent? Why?*

But then he remembered that she was an innocent

victim in the tug of war of power. He kicked them out of the house and warned them to stay away from her. Their hate was such that he wouldn't put it past them to suffocate her while she was sleeping. Marco didn't want them anywhere near her. Only those he trusted, those that had accepted her, were allowed close. Maria blamed herself. Marco couldn't blame anyone until she woke up and he would find out what happened to make her try to kill herself. Would life *with me be so bad? Did the thought of being close to me disgust her so much she didn't want to live anymore? I swear She was fine when I left her. So, what happened in between?* He watched the recording repeatedly and questioned Maria wanting to know every word they had said. Still, nothing made sense. Questions raced through his mind, as he waited for her to wake.

But Enzo needed help. The family needed their Don, so reluctantly he left Liz in the care of the doctor. Maria and Gino, who was adamant he wouldn't take his eyes off her. Marco assumed Gino felt guilty that she tried to kill herself while on his watch. He knew she was in safe hands. Although she was in the back of his mind, he always went straight to her room, before crashing alone in his bed. Exhausted by the amount of work, calls and paperwork that had piled up, he refused help from his second and locked himself away while he concentrated on his mafia.

Three weeks he waited for any movement to show that she was alive, but nothing changed and so life went back to normal. He did his hours and then spent some time with Liz before sleeping and starting his day again.

Two slow months had passed when he got the call. His queen was finally awake.

CHAPTER NINE

THE RAT

The first emotion Liz felt when she woke up was confusion which soon turned to disappointment as she looked around her, which then turned to fear. *Fuck! That didn't go as planned.* She tried to wipe her eyes, but her wrists were shackled by brown leather restraints. "What the fuck?" *Now I'm in trouble.* Liz stared at the red raised tissue of the scar as a reminder that she failed to take her life. Liz also noticed her nails has started growing back which made her wonder how long she'd been asleep.

Marco came into the room around five that afternoon. He looked tired and stressed and Liz knew she was the cause. *There's no way he would understand why I did it. He has no conscience when it comes to hurting or killing someone. He's mafia he has no empathy.* But she would rather use Marco as a therapist than speak to a total stranger. He sat beside the bed and wouldn't look her in the eye. For ten minutes he gave her the silent treatment when Liz had enough and spoke out.

"They will be coming for me."

Finally, he turned his head, but his face held an angry, dangerous expression.

"I know," he growled. "Do you think I care?" He then took a deep breath and held onto one of Liz's shackled wrists. "Is that why you did it? Why you tried to leave me?" His voice held a tender tone and it broke Liz's heart to hear it.

"No – I mean yes." Liz stuttered and then stared at the white ceiling as tears dripped down her face. And she couldn't even brush them away.

Without needing to see him, she told Marco what happened at the banquet and then blamed him for the death of her mother and the innocents.

"And you think, all of that was your fault? You've taken on the weight of responsibilities of all those dead onto your shoulder. No wonder you felt so depressed. But why did you not talk to me about it? Oh, my dear silly girl."

He stood up and over the bed where she was trapped. Gently he wiped her face with his hands and then bent down and softly kissed her lips.

"I wish you had talked to me before you reached the point where you couldn't go on." He said sadly, as he undid the restraints, and she was able to put her arms around him.

"Those people died because of me and when they come, and they will come for both of us, more people will die. I just can't have that on my conscience."

"First you have nothing to do with the bombing in Greece. That's on me. Well, Nicolo, he got a little carried away."

"A little," Liz screeched. "He blew away those innocent workers, my cousins, he even killed my mother. Okay, she wasn't a great role model and didn't have much love for me and even faked her death, leaving me to grieve for years, but she was still my mother."

"Then I'm sorry for your loss and all those deaths that you blame on yourself, but it isn't your fault. Things happen. People die, especially in this business and yes, more people will die and that is how life goes. I don't expect to live a long life, Mia Caro. Every time I leave the house, I know it could be the last. But I've accepted this. This is how mafia men live. And if you think for one moment I'm scared of the Russians or Greek coming after me, then you need to understand that I have enemies all over the world. I run the biggest mafia family in Europe. I run Italy."

"I know, Don."

"Call me Marco when we're alone. I love hearing my name coming from your lips."

"Marco, I know you run a powerful mafia, but do you think the Russians or Greeks will attack alone? They will join forces. My father wants me dead, without me he has no heir. If he dies, I take over the Greek mafia. And Yuri — wants me as a wife to abuse and rape whenever he likes." Tears started running again.

Marco held her tight.

"I will never let that happen. Promise me you will never try to take your life again." He lifted her chin. "Or do I have to have you committed like the family wants?"

Liz gasped and shook her head. "No, I promise it will never happen again." She tried to lay her head on his chest, but he took her chin again and raised her head.

"And do you promise that you will come to talk to me anytime you're upset, feeling down, depressed or suicidal again?"

His grip tightened on her chin.

"I promise. I'm sorry Marco, for all the trouble I have caused. But I'm not worth fighting a war over. I'm no one special. I don't understand why everyone wants me. I'm nothing."

Marco stood up and started pacing the room. Then rushed to the bed, and Liz moved over in fright. "Don't you ever say that again. You're not nothing. You are everything, especially to me."

Liz shook her head in denial. "When they come, people will die and I'm not worth a mafia war."

"And when they come, we will be ready." The Don tone was back. There was no arguing with him, even though Liz tried.

"You can't take the Greek and the Russian mafia on. I know you hold power, but they will be too many, even for you. And I won't allow you to fight for me, Marco. I won't allow any more to die."

He laughed but it was a sarcastic laugh. "And you think I would listen to you. You think you have the right to tell me, the Don of the Italian mafia, what to do?"

He grabbed Liz's wrists and started to wrap the restraints around her again.

"No, please. Marco don't." Liz cried.

"I have to leave and do something, and I don't trust you not to harm yourself again. I will be back shortly and then we will talk more. Don't be upset, Mia Caro. I love you and I promise no one will hurt you ever again, including yourself." He kissed her forehead and then turned and walked out of the door.

No one else visited her and she assumed that was

Marco's order. So, she slept with both wrists still in restraint. But when she woke, she was curled up on her side, both arms tucked into her body. Marco was standing by the door talking quietly to Nicolo, when Nicolo motioned his head to her and Marco turned, whispered something to him before coming over to Liz's bed.

"They are letting you leave tomorrow. But you'll be on 24/7 watch until I can trust you again."

"Who is babysitting me?" Liz asked,

"Nicolo and Sara."

Liz sat up in bed in alarm. "You can't do that to me. They hate me."

"Liz, Nicolo saved your life. Did you know you have a rare blood type, and you were going to die if we didn't find a match? Nicolo saved your life."

"Why did he do that?" she asked.

"Because I ordered him to, and everyone follows my orders or suffers the consequences."

Liz huffed, "Their words hurt me, but I wouldn't kill myself because of it. I'm not that weak."

Liz sat up in bed and reached for the water. After a couple of sips, she put the glass down and stared at the man sitting beside her bed, caressing the scar on her right hand.

"Marco, you have to let me go." He raised his head, eyebrows were up, and he was wide-eyed. She knew she needed to make him understand. "I'm no good for you. I will bring trouble to you, your door, and your mafia family. You don't need it and I'm not worth it."

'Let me make one thing very clear to you, ragazza ingenua. (Naive girl) I own Italy. I am the boss of every Capo around Italy. If I tell them to jump off a cliff, they will do it or face a bullet. If I tell them to prepare for a war with the Greeks and the Russians, they wouldn't dare question it. I'm not going to tell you how many Capos and soldiers are under my orders, but just know the moment the Greek or Russian mafia show their hand, they will be exterminated for good."

A chill ran through Liz's body as she thought of the unnecessary deaths, again for her sake.

"Why would they give up their lives for me, just because you order them to?" she asked.

"They wouldn't for you. But they would for their queen." Marco knelt on one knee and took out a black box from his suit pocket. "I wouldn't have left you earlier, but as you see, I needed to go shopping." He laughed and then turned serious. "Liz Finely, will you do me the honour of becoming my wife and sit upon the throne beside me?"

"What are you doing?" Liz gasped and covered her mouth with her hands, "You're crazy. You don't even know me."

"I know that I love you, and we will get to know each other. I know my family will fight to the death for their queen and I know that Yuri won't go near you once we are married. And I know that when I put a bullet in your father's head, we will rule Greece together."

"So, this marriage is to benefit both of us. It doesn't matter that I don't love you?"

"You will in time."

"A marriage of convenience then?" She folded her arms stubbornly.

"I will live by the wedding vows I say to you, and I hope you will do the same, Elizabeth."

"You're crazy," she said and giggled.

They stared at one another as though they were trying to read each other's emotions and the longer they were transfixed, the closer their heads came until their lips touched, and it wasn't a kiss of passion.

It was slow, meaningful and Liz felt as though he was giving her everything into the kiss. The promise to keep her safe, the promise of fidelity and the promise that he would respect her. When she needed to take a break from the long-lasting emotional kiss, she unwantedly pulled away. Both were panting hard and rested their foreheads together.

"So, is that a no?" he asked. Making them both laugh,

Liz sighed." I don't know why you think I'm worth all this trouble, or why you would want to be stuck with me for the rest of your life. But Marco Lucianno – shit, I must be crazy." She took a deep breath. "Marco Lucianno, I accept your offer of marriage and I pray you never regret your decision."

Marco took the pink diamond ring out of the box and placed it on her finger. Not surprisingly it fit. He stood up, pulling Liz off the bed and wrapped his arms around her as he leaned down and kissed her passionately.

"I will never let anything hurt you again. I never want to see your tears. You're my queen and will be treated as one."

***

Liz didn't know how she would be treated by the rest of Marco's family. But the moment she walked inside after Marco, the butlers and maids all bowed and addressed her as madam. Many of the Capos who had been seated in the lounge waiting for their arrival, met them in the hall and congratulated them both on their engagement and took Liz's hand kissing it and swore to protect her, and addressed as their queen. Liz was overwhelmed and didn't know which way to look and how to reply to this sudden change in their behaviour.

Marco must have noticed how uncomfortable she was as she felt him take her arm and supporting her, they walked up the stairs towards their room. Liz sighed deeply when she entered and sat on the bed. The whole day had exhausted her emotions and all she wanted to do was curl up with her fiancé and sleep. But that never happened. Once Liz was settled, he kissed her forehead and excused himself, leaving Maria and Liz alone. Marco wasn't kidding when he said she would be on a 24/7 watch. She couldn't believe it when she heard a click of a lock and knew that he had locked them in.

If the camera wasn't enough, now she would have Maria watching her like a hawk. Although feeling aggravated about the situation, Liz was relieved that she wasn't locked in a room with Sara instead.

After Liz was settled back in bed. Maria bought a chair over to the side and sat down with her arms folded as she stared at Liz.

"I don't know why you felt the need to do what you did. But I understand you must have had a good reason. I don't expect to ever learn what the reason is. But know that I am here for you as your maid and friend and if you ever need to talk, know I am a good listener."

Liz reached out and took one of Maria's hands. "Thank you. I appreciate that."

"The Don has left strict instruction for me and rules for you, which I will tell you about now."

Liz huffed as she waited to hear what Marco was going to do to her next.

"I am to accompany you to the bathroom for when you bathe. You will not find any sharp instruments inside the bathroom and the mirror has been taken out."

Liz gasped and folded her arms as Maria continued.

"Breakfast and lunch will be bought up here, but you will need to be downstairs every evening for dinner. When you leave the room for exercise you will be accompanied by two guards every time, you're in the room, the door will be locked, and you need to tell your guard if you require anything."

"Jeez, this place is getting more like a prison. I thought being the fiancé of the Don, would give me a little more room to breathe."

"Of course, it does. It will once the boss trusts you not to hurt yourself again."

I wonder how long he's going to keep me under guard. How do I build that trust back up?

"Umm, I think I should tell you that Sara will be taking over when my shift ends."

Liz groaned and threw her head into her hands.

"I think this will be good for you both. Time to talk and for her to make amends."

Liz sat up. "You heard?"

"After what she said, it soon spread around the staff."

Liz groaned again. "She hates me. I wouldn't be surprised if she tries to suffocate me with a pillow while I sleep"

Liz was being serious, but Maria took it as a joke and sniggered. She then pointed to the camera. "Someone is always watching."

"Any more rules I need to know about?"

"Not for now. You should rest, madam. I will be just over here if you need anything."

Liz watched Maria get settled in a chair by the window and saw her pull out a small book from her apron pocket. Liz's eyes were closing and so she laid her head down on the pillow and fell straight into a deep sleep.

When Liz woke and opened her eyes, her heartbeat so fast as she saw Sara standing beside her, with scorn on her face.

"You know you should have told me you were going to commit suicide. I would have helped hold the blade steady and made sure you did the job right."

Liz gasped. "Why are you so cold? What have I done to make you hate me?"

"Oh, now. Let me see—" Sara stood in front of the bed and counted on her fingers. "One, you are a British spy who has wormed their way into our mafia family. I know what your game is, and you will have your throat cut before I allow you to hurt my family. Two, you are a Greek whore, again, spying for your father and forcing Marco to believe your lies. But you don't fool me.

"You are a pitiful tramp. A whore who I'll never respect. You have everyone fooled but not me. I doubt that you ever wanted to kill yourself. You just did it to get sympathy from Marco. And Marco does like the ladies, especially those that open their legs so freely."

Liz couldn't stop the tears from falling and covered her mouth as she choked back her sobs.

"Pathetic!" Sara spat. "If the camera wasn't on, I would throttle you with my own bare hands. You don't belong here. You don't deserve to breathe the same air as Marco. So, do us all a favour and next time you try to kill yourself, do it right!"

Liz knew she had to stand up for herself otherwise Sara would continue to bully her mentally until she had no more strength left, and she promised Marco she wouldn't try to take her life again.

Wiping her eyes, she sat up against her pillows. "How dare you judge me? You don't know me. You don't know the hell I have been through before being kidnapped by the Italian Mafia. But Marco knows the truth and he believes me. He would know if I was lying. He wouldn't have invited me to the table if he didn't trust me. He wouldn't have tried to save my life if he didn't care for me." Liz took a deep breath before finishing with her big finale. "And he wouldn't have asked me to marry him if he didn't love me." She said waving her ring finger in Sara's face.

"Why you little witch! What spell have you put on the Don? He doesn't love you; you fool. He's using you, as he does with every female he fucks. You are just a commodity to him, and he will make sure he gets his payment in full before you are thrown back into the caring arms of your real fiancé."

Liz gasped. Sara smirked. "Oh, yes, Yuri Ivanhov knows exactly where you are. Oh, and by the way, I'm doubtful Marco has mentioned this to you, but you are on the most wanted list by the MI5, MI6, and FBI. Apparently, there were no survivors to speak about what happened at the banquet in London and you were not among the bodies. I should really contact them and let them know your location. Seems everyone wants a piece of the darling Greek princess."

"Do you know what you have done?" Liz cried out.

Sara ignored her and continued with her rant. "So, don't get too comfortable. There's no way you will be walking down that aisle. Forget those stupid dreams. You think you've been to hell. Princess, hell is coming to you and that's a promise."

A knock on the door stopped Sara from further verbally attacking Liz's mental state. Liz watched Sara's demeanour change from anger to calm like a switch of a button before she opened the door.

"Boss wants you in the office," Mario told her.

"But I'm supposed to be watching his fiancé," she said calmly.

"He's asked me to stay with her until your return. I would hurry, Sara. You know the Boss doesn't like being kept waiting."

Mario watched her run down the steps before closing the door and then turning to Liz.

"Madam, the Don has asked me to remind you that it's time to take your anxiety medicine. And if you don't mind me saying, you seem as though you need it. Are you okay, do you want me to fetch the boss?"

Liz's breath shuddered before shaking her head and answering no. Mario watched her take the pill and then she turned her back on him and curled up. Feeling exhausted and as though a weight was pulling her body down into the bed, her eyes fluttered closed.

Mario sighed heavily and sat on the chair by the win-dow and watched her sleep.

CHAPTER TEN
PRETTY WOMAN

What Sara didn't know was that there was now audio along with the camera feed and most of the male family, minus Nicolo, who had been sent on an errand watched and listened to Sara's threats, giving herself over as a rat. She had broken the Omerta. She had broken the families' trust, and the men knew exactly what would happen next, each of them feeling their rage and want for revenge.

Once Sara was shot and killed, Marco called a meeting. Maria sat in the same chair Mario had vacated and opened her book and started reading as Liz continued to sleep.

Marco sat up straight and stared into the faces of his men.

"So, we know the Russians are coming, or are already here, either alone or with the Greeks. We need to inform our allies and make sure our backs are covered."

Enzo spoke out. "She will need to be announced before they will stand with you."

Marco stood up, leaned over his desk, and growled. "They will stand with me or suffer the consequences. I am their king, the Don, and to disobey me and refuse an order will mean death. Yet, I agree that announcing our engagement and allowing them to see Liz's beauty and character shine, will satisfy them, I'm sure."

"She will make a formidable queen. She's feisty and still has a caring soul, after what she's been put through. We are happy for you, Boss."

Agreements rang through the room.

"But – "Stefano said. "Even being the next heir to the Greek throne, she's never lived a mafia life. She doesn't know how we live, what risk she will be taking and what might happen if she's attacked by one of our many enemies. This will be a new world to her and forgive me for speaking negatively, I just don't see her being strong enough for this life. Already she had tried to kill herself. I understand why she did it, that it was out of guilt. Marco, if you are certain she is the one and will stand by your side and be the strong and deadly queen you deserve, then you have my oath." Stefano bowed his head and hoped he wouldn't find a knife at his throat or a bullet in his chest, for speaking out of turn.

"You forget that she trained and worked as an agent for MI5. If they believed she could do that job, then I do not doubt she is capable of a lot more than she's shown. However, it may take a while for her strength to grow. This is down to us and the beating and torture she went through and then the guilt of all those her father killed. It will take time and training from us all to get Liz back to the mental and physical condition she once was. And in answer to your question, Stefano, I couldn't imagine anyone else by my side. Also, remember what we gain with this union?"

"So, are you all willing to lay down your life for us, for her?"

A choir of shouts of agreements echoed through the room. Marco smiled and sat back down in his chair. The others did the same.

Stefano coughed to gain attention, "What about Nicolo?"

"Don't worry about him. I will speak to him." Marco answered.

"But do we trust him?"

Marco was silent for a while before he spoke. "Although he is my brother, his wife was a rat, and he has shown nothing but disdain for Elizabeth. Can I trust him? Only time will tell. Act normal around him. I will keep him busy and away from her. But watch him closely, especially now."

Everyone mumbled their agreement, and some bowed their heads down.

"So, Enzo, get in touch with the Capos and organize a dinner. Don't let them know why. Make sure they know they are obligated to attend. Elizabeth is to know nothing. She is coping with enough as it is. I want her kept completely in the dark. Once they have met their Queen and oaths have been sworn, then we will move her to one of the safehouses. For now, double the guards. Make sure the perimeter is secured. No one comes in and out without my approval. Am I clear?"

"Si, Capo." They chorused.

Marco took a sip of his whisky and laid back in the chair. A comfortable silence settled over the room until Maria started yelling for the Boss.

Marco jumped off his chair and ran to the door. Enzo and Carlos were already running up the stairs when he joined them. As soon as he heard Liz's shouting and whimpers, he knew he could handle it from there.

"I've got this." He told his men as they attempted to crowd the door trying to see inside.

"Get back to your jobs. Maria, you can leave too. I can take care of her. I'll call you if I need anything."

Everyone did as they were told and started walking back down the stairs, Marco shut the bedroom door and made his way over to Liz who was thrashing in the sheet, as sweat glistened her skin. The first thing he did was remove her soaked nightdress that clung to her skin. Then getting a wet, cool flannel from the bathroom he laid it on her forehead as he wrapped the sheet around her body and cradled her in his arms while speaking to her softly. Only the words she cried out unnerved him. He realised maybe he wasn't the right person to be attending her and wake her from the night terrors when it was his mafia's torture, that made her scream and beg to be let go, that she knew nothing about her father's warehouse.

Her whimpering turned into Italian and as he rocked her and whispered words hoping to calm her. She called out his name begging him not to hurt her. His heart fell to his stomach. *How can such an innocent woman fall in love with a man like me, especially after my treatment of her?* "But I can't let you go, Mia Caro. There are too many people out to hurt you worse than me and I swore to protect you. So, you are mine. One day I hope you can forgive me for what I did to you. You have no idea what you mean to me. How just your presence brightens up my day, my life. Call me selfish but I can't let you go. I need you just as much as I need air. You're my light. Things will get better from now on, I give you my promise, Mia Caro

Her body shook and all that could be heard was sniffing and tiny hiccups as she fell asleep in his arms.

***

Liz woke up to strong arms holding her tight. *Are we moving too fast? What am I talking about? I just accepted his proposal of marriage. I must be mad.* Liz bit her lip as she tried to decide whether to just lay where she was and not move or turn towards him. That decision was out of her hands when Marco's husky voice made her shiver for all the right reasons.

"I know you are awake, darling. I can hear the cogwheels of your mind working double time."

Liz turned over and faced him. She reached out her hand and caressed his soft cheek. Then not waiting for him to make the first move, she snuggled closer and kissed his soft lips. Marco moved his head back, and surprise was written on his face.

Shit, well that went well. She was about to apologise when Marco grabbed hold of her body and turned her over, so he was on top of her and then kissed her lips hard. Opening her mouth, their tongues battled it out, wanting to touch and taste everywhere. Liz held her arms around his neck, spread her legs open and deepened their kiss. Feeling his hard erection pushing against the thin material of her nightdress, she knew he was trying to get inside her. She was wet below and knew that Marco could feel it too.

"I want you, Liz. I want to fuck you hard and rough and take what has always been mine."

Just his words made her even wetter, and that want now burned inside her needed quenching.

"Then take what belongs to you, Don Marco," she answered breathlessly.

Marco sat her up and pulled off her nightdress, undid her bra. In less than a few seconds, she was almost naked. Marco stood up and got off the bed. She watched him pull down his boxers and display his hard, thick cock that was dripping with pre-cum. Her mouth watered as she watched him walk slowly towards the bed. Then Marco stopped and pointed his finger at her, directing her to come to him. Liz stood up and walked around the bed until she was standing in front of him.

"On your knees."

Just his command could have made her orgasm. Turned on by his dominant nature, she fell to her knees, looked up at him and smiled before taking his length into her mouth.

His gasps and groans were exactly what she wanted to hear as she went to work on him, sucking and licking. Her hair was grabbed, and she was pulled off and forced to look at him.

"Open your mouth wide," he ordered.

Keeping his hand tight, on her hair, he fucked her mouth, pushing himself deep down into her throat making her gag. He continued with pushing her to the limits until she was out of breath before pulling her off and then shoving his cock inside her warm, wet mouth again.

Liz allowed him to use her mouth. She would permit him to use her any way he wanted. Just knowing he wanted her and how he reacted to her, was enough to submit fully to him. She felt his cock start to pulsate and knew he was going to cum. She was ready to take him all. To taste him and relished in the thought, but he pulled away just before.

"Get on the bed. Lie on your back, keep your legs open and don't move." He instructed.

Wiping the dripping saliva from her mouth, she stood up and did what he told her to do. Liz never had a problem showing off her body, especially with the way he was watching her, like prey. As he licked his lips, she knew that he was ready for dessert.

***

Liz opened her eyes as she felt butterfly kisses on her neck and collarbone. Fucked into exhaustion, she didn't realize she had fallen back to sleep. Where he got his stamina, she didn't want to know. Just thinking about how experienced he was, knowing where to touch and lick and getting her to the point of no return, only to then to stop and refuse her to cum. When he finally whispered the words and gave her permission to let go, she'd never had such a strong orgasm in her life. She'd never squirted before, but the sheet she was laying on was wet from the sex they had all night.

As Liz got out of bed, and her feet touched the carpeted floor, they collapsed on her, and she fell to her knees groaning.

"Are you okay, down there?" She heard the laughter in his voice.

"A little help, please." She replied as she scowled at him.

He picked her up in his arms and carried her into the bathroom, while she sat watching him run a bath.

"After you have soaked and had something to eat, we will be going out. I will have Maria pick something for you to wear."

"Do we have to, Marco?" She pouted. "Can't we just stay in bed and watch movies all day."

He smiled at her and held his hands out as she carefully stepped into the bubbles and warm water. When she submerged her body, and the water hit her sore pussy, she breathed a sigh of relief.

Marco climbed in and sat behind her, pulling her against him so she was laying between his legs and resting her back and head on his chest. He gently washed her body with a flannel while kissing and sucking on her neck.

"How I would love to spend the day making love to my beautiful fiancé…" The words made her stomach flutter. "I still have a mafia to run, and you shouldn't overdo it. You're not well yet."

Liz whipped her head around and stared at him open-mouthed. "You didn't seem to care about that earlier."

"I know the signs. I was keeping watch. I think I know what your limits are while you're not well. But once we get you back to a healthy weight and start training, you'll soon be able to keep up with me."

Liz knew it wasn't said in arrogance but was the truth, and she was determined to prove him right. She turned all the way around and straddled him as she took the flannel and washed his neck and chest.

"Come," he said after kissing her. "Breakfast, and then we need to leave."

When they left the bathroom dressed in only white Egyptian cotton bathrobes, there was a table set for them on the balcony with sweet pastries, eggs, bacon, juice, and fruit salad.

Liz followed Marco and sat down opposite him. They were both silent as they ate. Marco was scrolling and typing on his phone as Liz sat munching on a slice of peach when she sighed. Marco took his attention off his phone and smiled.

"That was either a bored or contented sigh," he said.

"This is the first time I have felt safe and happy in such a long time," she answered.

Marco took Liz's hands. "I once told you that I never feel regret, especially with how you were treated here. Well, I was wrong. If I could take back any moment of my life and redo it, it would be that."

"And how would you redo it, Don Marco?" she asked as she stroked his hand.

"Oh, I would have still kidnapped you, but I would have dealt with your torture myself."

Liz tried to move her hand, but as if he was expecting that, he held onto her wrist tightly. "I would have tortured you sexually for days on end until I got what I wanted."

Liz pulled her arm away from him, knocking over a glass of juice in the process. "So, you would have killed me anyhow, as I know nothing. Death by sex, I suppose it's not a bad way to go."

She stood up and tried to leave the balcony, but he grabbed hold of her and pulled her chin up, so she faced him.

"My sweet darling, I was only joking with you. I promised you I would not hurt you or allow anyone to hurt you again, and I will make good on my promise. Now, hurry and dress, it's late, and we need to leave."

"Where are we going?"

"To buy you a new dress," he answered, as he zipped up his trousers.

"Marco, I can't go out," she cried.

Worried by her change in tone, he walked over to her and held her in his arms. "What is wrong, my darling."

"I can't go out, look," Liz cried as she held out her scarred wrists and arms. "No matter how much I love shopping and I'm in need of some retail therapy, I'm not in the state where I can go out and be seen like this."

Marco bought each wrist to his lips and kissed them gently. "I will find the finest surgeon and we will get these scars removed." He then pressed a number on his phone before telling the person to bring him a pair of long white cotton gloves. He went inside the walk-in wardrobe and picked a long black, sleek, maxi skirt and matched it with a white silk blouse and then laid them in her arms.

"Hurry," he urged.

Within minutes, there was a knock on the door, and Marco returned to Liz holding white gloves that matched the outfit perfectly.

"Where did all these clothes come from? How did you know my size?"

"I had my personal shopper bring them. But know each item I chose myself."

"Grazia." She ran to him and hugged him tightly, as he gently patted her back and kissed her head.

"I have never been treated like this before in my life," she gushed.

"You, my darling, were born a princess and will soon be my queen, so get used to being pampered and spoilt. You deserve anything and everything. Money is no object."

"No, I wouldn't do that. I'm not that kind of girl."

He held her shoulders and gazed into her eyes. "I know you're not. That's why I'm in love with you, Elizabeth. I've never met someone like you. You showed how caring you are when the guilt ate you up for the massacre your father created. You showed me in the office that time, how feisty you can be. You'll soon learn when you can bring that feistiness out and when it's the wrong time to say anything. And you're so strong, to have gone what you've been through and still be standing and still be giving me attitude. You're the woman I've been looking for to stand by my side and be my Queen. I know you don't feel that way right now, but you'll be taught how to act, what to say in certain situations, although I doubt if you're listening, and that's what I love about you. Under this weak persona, you're showing I know that you are more. And although I haven't seen you fight or shoot a gun, I do not doubt that you can hold your own. I even bet that once the true Liz is back, you could beat Gino in a match."

Liz giggled.

"You have all the attributes I have been wanting in my queen."

Liz didn't know what to say. She gulped and then smiled again. "It's a good job we found each other, then."

She watched his face drop and then returned a tight smile before asking if she was ready to leave.

Liz put on some nude-coloured shoes but didn't bother taking a bag as she had nothing to put in it. Marco also realised this and promised they would pick up toiletries, make-up and whatever else she needed.

Before they left the bedroom, Liz took his arm. "Umm

Marco, I know I'm falling for you and hard, but I'm not quite there yet. I'm sorry."

"My sweet girl," Marco replied as he kissed her lips softly. "I never expected for you to say it back. Not with what I did to you. With everything, you've been through, I know it will take time for you to trust me. I'm satisfied with you falling. Just know I will be there to catch you."

They kissed passionately before pulling away, grinning at each other. As she opened the door, he said in Italian and quietly "Oh, woman, you have no idea what you're doing to me." Liz heard, and that made the butterflies in her stomach flutter yet again.

As she walked down the stairs and watched Marco giving orders to his men, she wondered how a powerful mafia man could cause her to feel like a teenager again.

***

The first store the car stopped at was one that she'd pass by anytime. She wouldn't even bother to glance in the window. This was for the rich and privileged, carrying only designer labels. A carrier bag probably cost ten euros in a place like this. But she took Marco's hand and took a deep breath before stepping out of the car. The moment she entered the store she felt out of place. It didn't matter that her clothes and shoes were designer names, she didn't feel like she was welcome. *Probably wondering what Marco was doing with someone like me. It's obvious I stick out like a sore thumb.* She watched the bimbos crowding around Marco, smiling their Botox lips at him.

"La mia fidanzata sta cercando un vestito per una cena formale, lungo, nero ma non troppo scoperto"

(My fiancé is looking for a dress for a formal dinner: long, black, sexy but not too revealing.)

The head sales assistant took Liz around the back while Marco sat with a whisky in his hand, while he scrolled through his phone. Ten minutes had passed and instead of Liz coming out in one of the dresses they had found for her, she came out dressed in her day outfit and walking over to Marco, she whispered timidly that she wanted to leave.

"Are you, okay? You look so pale and sick," he asked.

"Please just get me out of here." There were unshed tears in her eyes, but the last thing she wanted was to give them the satisfaction of seeing her cry. She had humiliated herself enough for one day.

Marco sat in the back seat and helped Liz as she tried to get her breathing under control before she went into a full-blown panic attack. Once she was able to speak coherently, she told him what had happened. He hugged her once more before stepping out of the car, getting his phone out and having a heated conversation with someone on the other end. Liz's eyes closed from exhaustion. So, she never saw what he did next.

He went back into the shop and walked over to the blonde who was supposed to have helped Liz, he raised the flat of his hand and smacked her across the cheek.

"How dare you disrespect my fiancé like that! If she wasn't waiting for me, I would blow your fucking brains out. Hand me your phones now!"

The three girls inside gave over their phones while Marco went through them until he found what he was searching for. Just then, a little lady entered the store and rushed over to Marco.

"Please, Mr Lucianno forgive me for the disrespect you and your fiancé have suffered. Let me sort out an arrangement of dresses that your fiancé can try on in the privacy of your own home. And you can send the others back when it is convenient for you and please allow me to gift the dress your fiancé chooses as an apology for the way you have both been treated. Congratulations on your engagement,"

"That is acceptable. The blame is not with you, and we have been friends for a long time, Rose."

Marco held up the phone and made sure all could see the picture. Rose covered her mouth with a gasp.

"My fiancé has been to hell and back and she wears these scars to prove it. How dare you take a photo without her knowledge and then have the nerve to gossip about her. You better pray you haven't sent the photograph anywhere."

The blonde quickly shook her head.

Marco crushed each mobile phone under his foot and then turned to the shop workers.

"And you better leave town, because if we meet up again, I may be forced to rearrange your face. Do you understand?"

"Yes, Mr Lucianno." All three girls answered.

Rose scowled at the women before walking with Marco to the car.

"Again, my apologies, sir, and thank you for allowing me to make amends." She said as she handed over the dress bags to the driver.

"It is a shame that our business has ended like this. I doubt my fiancé would want to come back here again. Take care of yourself, Rose."

Marco quietly got into the back seat of the car and when he saw Liz had fallen asleep, he lowered her down, so her head rested in his lap. As he stroked her hair, he thought back to how her father could torture and whip his daughter so viciously that it tore the skin and left a permanent scar. As he thought about the pain, he would put her father through, he remembered that Nicolo had been part of the men interrogating her. If he had known they were administering her punishment to get her to talk, and that Nicolo had whipped her, he would have stopped such treatment immediately. Now the scars that she wears is the trigger for her PTSD and it could have been in Italy and not Greece where she was brutally marked. He shook his head as he tried to deny the truth.

"Never again will you suffer such treatment. I will make it up to you, even if it takes me forever." He lovingly caressed Liz's cheek.

Liz was down for the count. Her body had suffered so much stress over the last weeks that exhaustion and not eating right, caused her to shut down again.

Marco carried her into the house, up the stairs and laid her on the bed, throwing a thin blanket over her. He turned to the driver, who was standing outside their bedroom door, holding the dress bags. Marco thanked him and hung the dresses up in the closet and quietly left the room.

***

He went to the office and called for Luca and Stefano. Enzo, who he also wanted to speak to, was already in the office, going through papers.

"Is everything okay? I saw you carrying Elizabeth to her room. Did she faint again?"

Enzo's question rubbed Marco the wrong way and so he didn't answer him. When Stefano and Luca appeared, he told Luca to lock the door. Each of the Capos eyed one another and knew something was going to go down.

Marco sat back in his chair and stared at his men one at a time. "Before we begin, I want full disclosure and I promise that there will be no reprimand for your honesty."

The men all nodded.

"The three of you and Nicolo who isn't here for reasons you will learn shortly oversaw the interrogation of Elizabeth. I want you to tell me what happened from the moment she was incarcerated."

The men gave their account on what they took part in, but when Luca mentioned that Nicolo offered to handle the rest of the interrogation, Marco stopped him there. "You all knew about this?"

"Si," they answered.

Marco rubbed his temples. "So, let me get this straight, Nicolo was left alone with her for all the rest of the days she was imprisoned?"

Stefano gulped. Luca nodded.

Enzo folded his arms and said, "What is this all about, Marco? Has the princess been complaining about her treatment?"

He laughed, then went quiet when no one else thought it was funny.

"Let me tell you something about your future queen. She single-handedly defeated six terrorists without one hostage being hurt. While the rest of her team were being held at gunpoint, she started knocking off the terrorists one by one, until she was injected with peanut oil and went into anaphylactic shock. And the plan to extract her from the wedding shop was supposed to be in and out, no one gets hurt unnecessarily, but what does Nicolo do? He bombs the place so everyone including her cruel mother was killed.

"As you know, no one was released from the banquet hall. Her sadistic father gunned down everyone, just so he could extract his daughter. She sacrificed herself to save lives. She is the most unselfish, genuine, strongest woman I have ever come across. And because of her illness, how she has behaved, what you've seen, you've already concluded that she is weak and probably don't feel she is a good fit for me."

Enzo tried to interrupt but Marco held up his hand to silence him.

"No, I don't need to hear your opinion. I have heard things and seen the looks from your faces that give the truth away."

"First, she took the blame for all the deaths in the UK. She felt the blood of all those innocents was on her hands. Then, there was the wedding shop explosion. Again, she kept the blame. With all that inside her, also knowing that her parents had sold her to the Russian sadist, Yuri Ivanhov. She was then tortured and interrogated when she knew nothing and was innocent. God damn it!" He banged his fist on his desk. "Just the guilt she must have been feeling, whether warranted or not, was enough to want to take her own life.

"She didn't feel she deserved to live. She didn't believe she had earned a happy ever after. And now she's suffering from PTSD. I assumed it was from her father's treatment of her. Now I'm not so sure."

Marco switched a button and a huge projection screen came down on the right of the wall and covered the bookshelf. His heart raced as he switched another button and the cell Liz had been incarcerated appeared on the screen.

The men had almost given a correct account of their actions, Marco forwarded the video until it was just Liz and Nicolo. She did nothing to warrant the starvation, the beatings, the whippings, and he watched the grimace on his men's faces as Nicolo rubbed salt in her cuts and laughed as she tried to scream, but her throat was so dry that only quiet screeches came out. It was when Marco watched Nicolo slice a lemon in half and walk behind Liz, that he switched off the video and closed his eyes. There was silence in the room. Marco got out of his seat and walked around, perching himself on the edge of his desk as he glared at his men.

"No weak woman would have survived that. From now on I expect her to be treated with the utmost respect. Make sure she is comfortable and happy and doesn't want or need anything. Address her as your queen, as this will soon come to pass.

She needs to get away from this house and the toxic environment if she is to recover and build back her strength, and I intend to take her away once we have wiped the Greek and Russian scum off the map. You asked me, Stefano if I trusted my brother, and my answer has changed. No, I do not. I want him out of this house and nowhere near Elizabeth. Make it happen."

Enzo nodded.

"What we have discussed goes no further. If it does get out, I know who I will be coming for."

Marco warned Enzo as he unlocked the door.

Enzo turned. "You both have my loyalty, trust and love until my final breath."

Marcos nodded as he watched Enzo's retreating body.

"Luca, how are arrangements going with the dinner?"

"Enzo told me only The Marchellos can't make it. All of the others have been confirmed."

"And their excuse?" Marco asked.

"Father is abroad and can't get back in time." Luca mimicked a child's voice.

And the children have nothing to do with the mafia."

Marco's eyebrows lifted. "Oh really? We will have to change that. Set something up please, Stefano. And is the safe house ready for your queen?"

"We are just finishing last-minute comforts for her. Security has been ordered and is ready when you are. Don, now that you have mentioned her mental and physical health, I think it may be wise to have medical supplies and even a live-in doctor at the safe house."

"Yes, I agree." Marco then squeezed the shoulder of Luca and Stefano. "If you need me, I will be upstairs giving TLC to my queen."

CHAPTER ELEVEN

MEETING THE FAMILY

Liz woke up in Marco's arms to the sound of someone yelling his name desperately. Only immediate family would be able to get away with that – maybe, she thought. Marco jumped off the bed, leaned down and kissed her, reassuring her not to worry, he'd take care of it and to rest. She was about to argue, but Marco sped out of the room as though his pants were on fire. The yelling outside continued, until the noise got quieter, fading away with the slamming of an office door.

Liz let her imagination play out what the shouting was all about until Marie walked in with a tray containing a pot of tea, cream and sugar and a plate of biscuits and, of course, her medication.

"Perfect timing." Liz sat up in bed. She frowned when Maria handed her the pills.

"I don't think I need these anymore."

Maria shook her head. "The doctor wants you to finish the treatment. The happiness euphoria you're feeling could just be the medication. You feel so high with happiness, you could burst?"

"Yes!" Liz cried out. "But it's not the pills. I'm truly happy."

Liz showed Maria the ring.

"I'm getting married. OMG, we have a wedding to plan!"

Maria laughed. "Slow down, you'll give yourself anxiety if you're not careful. We can start looking at wedding planners after the Associates' Dinner."

"Associates' Dinner, what's that?"

Liz watched Maria swallow nervously.

"It's not my place, madam. Ask the Don. I'm sure he'll be happy to explain it to you."

"Umm," Liz mumbled. "Well, at least you can tell me when it is."

Maria bit her lip and glanced at the camera before saying softly. "Tomorrow evening."

"Tomorrow?" Liz yelled.

"I need to get my hair and nails done before then. How soon, on such late notice, can you schedule appointments in this town?"

"Madam, please calm yourself. The Boss will have my head if you get into a state again. Everything has been scheduled. The manicurist and first hairdresser will be coming in the morning. Although I'm not sure it's a good idea to touch your nails as they are still healing.

"I won't leave this room unless my nails look amazing," Liz told her stubbornly.

"Very well," Maria sighed. "The second hairdresser and makeup artist will be arriving late afternoon. The Don wanted to make sure you had time to rest in between appointments. Now, after those two bits of excitement, you should try to rest and calm yourself. All the Don wants is for you to be safe and healthy again."

"Very well, but I doubt if I can sleep more. I feel very awake right now".

"That's probably the medication."

Maria covered Liz with a sheet and walked back over to her chair by the window.

****

Even though Liz was Marco's fiancé and future queen to the empire, her help, opinion, and orders were ignored. She had God knows how many people coming to dinner and although one day she would be the woman of the house, the cooks, and maids, all knew their job and had everything organised. It made her feel useless and unwanted.

Marco, although being buried under work was told about Liz's distress, and he cursed himself when he realised, he forgot to tell her about the introductory meal that evening. Leaving his office, he rushed up to their bedroom and found her pacing the floor while nibbling on her fingernails.

"If you continue ripping them off, you'll have no nails left," Marco said, and then realised how that statement could come across the wrong way.

Liz spun around and faced him, with her hands on her hips she scowled. "Well, it's a good job I have a manicurist coming later." Liz watched his eyebrows lift. "Yes, Maria filled me in on the appointments I have all day. The only thing I'm yet to be told is why?"

"*Caro*, I'm sorry I completely forgot to tell you about tonight. I have been stuck in the office, dealing with work, and forgot to tell you about the dinner. Come sit with me outside for a moment."

Even though Liz was angry with him, she took his outstretched hand and let him lead her to the table and two chairs on the balcony. He pulled out a chair and waited for her to sit before seating himself.

"Forgive me, darling, for not speaking to you about this. Tonight, we have some very important people coming to dinner. My Capos, my mafia family from around the world will be flying in for dinner, tonight.

Liz interrupted him. "Did you say they are flying in from around the world just to have dinner here?"

"We are the Italian mafia. You have no idea of our wealth. As I was saying, the main reason for this dinner is for them to be introduced to you as their future queen. After dinner, we will leave you ladies to entertain yourself while my men and I will discuss the coming war."

"Will it really come to that?" Liz asked and took his hands and held them tight.

"It has already begun, my love. But that is all you will know. Women have no place in mafia business. So, I warn you now, do not ask questions. Do not get involved in any discussions about mafia business. Leave your conversations to shopping and beauty products."

Liz stood up; her eyebrows creased with a frown.

"But what about the training you want me to do. To display to you that I'm capable of shooting a gun and killing someone. Why say that if all I am to you is a doll and heir of the Greek mafia.

"Mia Caro, you will be a lot more than just a trophy wife. The training is to prepare you for what might come.

Once word gets out that you are my Queen. My enemies will use you as a target to get to me."

"Well, they would be stupid to try."

Marco laughed and hugged her then pulled away and his face turned cold again.

"Elizabeth, tonight is very important. We need these Capos to agree to fight alongside us, for the cause, and to do that they need to meet you, to see if you're worth shedding blood for."

"But I don't want any more people dying because of me. I won't allow that."

Marco forced her chin up. "I wouldn't choose you as my queen if I didn't think you were capable of defending yourself and any of the family if it comes down to it. Your caring nature wouldn't allow a member of our family to be hurt. But if the Don has spoken, his orders will be carried out and the same goes to you, Elizabeth. You will look like a queen, hold yourself up like a queen, and show your manners. But if someone disrespects you and I give you the okay, you may stand up for yourself as my strong and feisty queen would.

"If you are ever challenged or put in a corner, you show them what you are capable of! Do you understand how important this dinner is? Do you understand what role you need to play?"

Liz nodded. "I do, Don. I will do my best to hold my tongue."

Marco growled before walking towards the bedroom door.

"And in the future," Liz called out, stopping Marco in his tracks. "I would prefer more notice, so I have time to prepare a menu for the chefs and to make sure all of silver and crystal is sparkling for our guests."

Marco turned around and stormed towards her. Liz stood her ground and wasn't about to step back like a scared mouse. He grabbed her face and crushed his lips to hers until they were in a passionate kiss.

"This is why I love you," Marco said, before pecking her lips and departing from the room, leaving Liz wondering what had just happened.

***

Liz managed to sneak down and peek at the dressed dinner table before any guests arrived. Nerves, as well as excitement, caused her stomach to churn as she counted the number of chairs that were seated on both sides of a long oblong table. Silver cutlery, crystal glasses and impressive flower arrangements covered the gold silk tablecloths. Liz was impressed, but that just made her anxiety increase, so she ran back upstairs to hide in her bedroom and finish getting ready.

Acrylic bright red nails matched the red silk ball gown she wore. Red stilettoes ankle-strapped shoes and a glossy red lipstick, all Marco's orders. Who was she to go against him? This dinner was so important, and she didn't want to embarrass him or let him down. Her hair had been high-lighted with golden strips, her hair was straightened, and then gentle waves curled at the tips. Eyelashes curled, eye-brows plucked and hours of sitting in a chair being prod-ded, pulled, and painted and the result was amazing. Liz thought her face would be caked with makeup with as much as they put on her, but her face appeared fresh and glowing and with her new hairstyle, she felt like a new woman. *A new start. I can do this. I've got this.*

As per the instruction of Marco, Liz stayed upstairs until all the guests had arrived and were sitting down at the extended table. She sat nervously on the edge of the bed listening to the laughter and chatter getting louder by the minute. She attempted to chew on her nails, then remembered they weren't real nails and so she sat on her hands. Her nerves were getting the best of her and so she stood up and paced the room before standing in front of the mirror and giving herself a pep talk. She was so inside her head, she never heard the door open, and realised Marco was standing beside her staring at her reflection.

"Oh jeez, you gave me a fright," she gasped and turned to face him.

Marco was holding open a large jewellery box where a stunning gold necklace with a garnet and diamond pendant sat on black velvet.

"Oh Marco, it's beautiful." She paused, staring down at her feet and then back at the stunning jewellery. "But would you be upset if I didn't wear this tonight?"

He slammed the box shut and threw it on the bed. She watched him take a deep breath. Liz assumed it was the first time someone had refused him. How many necklaces had he given to other women?

"Don Marco," She touched his face making sure he was watching her. "With your permission, I only want to wear one piece of jewellery and not take away from its beauty and meaning." She lifted her hand that displayed the engagement ring. His frown suddenly turned into a huge smile that lit up his eyes.

"How right you are. But, Cara, never turn down a gift from me again."

"Si, Don," she answered, and bowed her head.

He turned her around towards the mirror and held her waist as they both started at their reflection.

"You look sinful. You were already beautiful, but this just highlighted the best features. How do you feel, my love?"

"I'm nervous, Marco. But I'm ready to stand by your side and those that resist or don't agree to this match, then they will suffer my tongue and your wrath."

Marco laughed. "I wouldn't want to go against your tongue, however–" He moved closer, grabbing her hips. He pulled her to his body and kissed her. Pushing his tongue into her mouth so she had no choice but to open up to him, the kiss deepened, the heat rose, and it was Marco that pulled away. Reluctantly, she thought she saw him pout.

"If we don't leave now, I'll take you right here and we won't leave the room."

Liz tapped her fingers on her chin feigning thought. "Umm, as delightful as that sounds, I wouldn't want to piss off thirty Capos. That would not leave a very good impression."

Liz smiled, took his arm, and they silently left the bedroom and walked down the stairs. They both listened to the laughter and chatter that stopped as soon as they walked into the banquet hall. All heads turned to Liz and Marco as they slowly walked towards the table.

The guests stood up from their seats. Liz's heart was pounding, both from nerves and excitement. She'd never been regarded or treated with such respect, and she loved the new feeling.

There was silence so when Marco spoke everyone heard.

"If you are sitting here at my table, you are family. You are trusted and loved, and I would give my life for any one of you men and my oath to protect every one of the ladies present."

There were cheers, clinking of glasses and lots of sentiments thrown around.

Marco held up his other hand and everyone hushed. "Standing beside me is Elizabeth Finley, the only heir to the Greek mafia. She is my fiancé and soon to be your queen."

There were gasps, murmurs and overall shock and surprise on the faces of the dinner guests. The family who already knew and loved Liz stood up and walked over to the couple. Luca was the first to take Liz's hand and kissed her engagement ring.

"Donna, hai il mia amore e la mia parola sul fatto che ti proteggerò fino al mio ultimo respiro."

(Donna, you have my love and oath that I will protect you until my last breath.)

Liz smiled and nodded down at him.

Each of the Capos said their oaths and referred to her as the Donna, Queen of the Italian mafia.

Only the men swore their oaths. The women watched, some in awe and some with envy, Liz thought.

Once the oaths were sworn, Marco and Liz took their seats. Marco at the head of the table and Liz on the left of him. Once everyone was seated the food was bought out and they all tucked into the fine feast.

The men didn't talk shop in front of the ladies and so chatted about sports and politics, TV shows and actors. As the women gossiped about people Liz had never heard of, Marco smiled at her. She smiled back and then continued eating her food while listening to the different conversations.

"My love, I was just telling Mario that in a fight Spiderman would beat Batman?"

His statement was again deferred by Mario, who spoke real fast Italian, just to get his point across. Marco took Liz's hand and kissed it before saying,

"What do you think?"

There was silence. Liz noticed everyone was staring at her. Was it they were waiting for her answer or that it wasn't normal practice for a Don to involve in conversation with a female? Liz knew she still had a lot to learn.

She coughed to clear her throat, which captured everyone's attention. "Although Batman has lots of fast and fun toys to play with and Spiderman has nought but a sticky web coming from his palm, if the Don, my King, states that Spiderman will beat Batman in a fight, then I agree. The Queen should always stand by her King."

Enzo stood up and raised his glass. "To the King and Queen."

Everyone stood up and toasted.

Marco and Liz smiled and nodded. Marco leaned and whispered into her ear, "Nicely done." Then addressed the table. "Gentlemen, it is time. Ladies, if you will excuse us."

The men rose to their feet, some kissed their wives, girlfriends on the cheek. Marco took Liz's hands and pulled her to the side. "Remember if it gets too much, you can retire early. You've had a long day and your health comes before entertaining the Capos whores."

"Are they really whores?" Liz asked, astonished.

"Well, no, only a couple. Most come from mafia families and other upstanding families. I don't know how long we will be, so don't wait up."

"What about the women? I can't just leave them down here unchaperoned?" Liz asked.

"Don't worry. They have drivers waiting to take them home as soon as they are ready."

"Forgive me, Marco, there is still so much I have to learn."

"And you will, in time. Goodnight, my love."

Liz watched the men leave and then turned to the women.

"Okay, who needs a drink?" she called out.

Of course, there were maids to do the serving, but this way she could look each woman in the eye and get a feel for them. Another trick she was taught in MI5

As she was handing out margaritas to everyone, she heard a young voice talking about the possibility of a coming war.

"I didn't know it was common practice for the wives to discuss mafia business."

Liz turned to the girl who had been gossiping, but another woman standing beside the loud-mouthed girl spoke first.

"Donna, please forgive her for her foolish tongue. She is young and not used to our ways and I think she's probably had too much to drink."

"Hmm, I understand," Liz said and smiled at the girl before turning back around.

"Ha! So, Marco doesn't confide in you. Where's the trust?"

The women were trying to hush the girl up, but she got louder, as though she had a point to prove.

"My Richie tells me everything. Just the other day he bought me a ring that would put yours to shame."

Liz had enough but knew she had to be diplomatic, whilst dealing with a drunk.

"You say Ritchie talks to you about things that even the future mafia queen doesn't know?"

"Of course, he does. He loves me and trusts me."

"And is this while you're on your knees, I suppose?" Liz asked.

The others gasped and covered their mouths.

The mouthy blonde continued her rant. "I see the way you look down on me like you're better than us. But you're nothing but a Greek whore."

There were gasps again and shouts of pleas to forgive her, but they knew she had gone too far and nothing they could say could save her.

"What is your name?" Liz asked sweetly.

"Alisha."

"And your husband's name?"

"Oh, we're not married." She snorted. We've only known each other for a month.

"Is that so?" Liz mused. "And pray tell me, where you heard someone call the future queen of the Italian mafia, a whore?"

"Well, it's obvious with how many men took you when you were a prisoner. Richie said you were nothing to shout about. He'd had better. Makes me wonder how you keep Marco satisfied."

Liz had enough. *It's time I showed them that I'm capable of being the Queen of the Italian mafia. That I'm able to stand up for myself. That I'm not as weak as they think I am.* The sea of ladies parted as she stormed towards Alisha. Raising her hand, she struck the woman's face and watched her crumble to the floor.

"How dare you refer to the Don as though you are best buddies! How dare you come into my house and disrespect me in front of my family! Not one man raped me. Our mafia does not condone rape, especially not to female prisoners."

The crying and screeching Alisha was doing was enough to bring the men back into the room and Marco was furious.

Liz stepped over Alisha as she continued laying on the floor until her man picked her up and held her, trying to get some sense out of the girl. Liz ignored all the other Capos. She whispered something to Marco and then told him, she had to take care of this herself or lose face, and that would be disastrous for them both. He stepped back, showing the others that he was keeping out of it. Liz stood in front of Ritchie as he held on to Alisha as she continued to play the act of a victim.

Liz raised her hands and slapped him around the face. She knew that the other Capos were probably reaching for their guns. She hoped Marco would stop her from getting shot.

"How dare you come into my home, to my table with a whore you barely know on your arm! She has disrespected me and in doing so she has disrespected the Don. Do you think you have the right to disclose vital secret mafia business to this whore? Did she sign the Omerta?"

"No." He whispered.

"What was it that you just told your Donna? Why not look your Don in the eyes and repeat that?"

Liz stepped back knowing Marco would take care of the rest.

"Guards," Marco yelled and immediately the couple were held tight.

"You broke the Omerta, and you know what the penalty is – death. Take them away." Marco commanded.

Liz stepped up to him and whispered in his ear. He nodded and called for silence.

"Capos, can your queen have your attention for a moment longer?"

Liz stood up straight and made sure to grab their attention.

"No matter what you may have heard from rumours, or direct from Richie's mouth, no man and that certainly includes Richie, ever raped me or sexually assaulted me while I was held below. The only man who has touched me this way since I've been here is my fiancé. Now, please accept my humble apology for interrupting your meeting. I assure you it will not happen again."

Liz tugged on Marco's jacket, knowing she wouldn't be able to stay on her feet for much longer and she didn't want anyone to witness her weakness.

"Enzo, continue the meeting. I will be with you momentarily."

Enzo nodded and ushered the men out of the banquet room and back into the office.

Liz collapsed in his arms before they were halfway up the stairs. He told Maria to discreetly call the doctor in to look at his fiancé knowing she had been put through a lot of stress for someone with her condition.

"Maybe it's time we got you a therapist and get this under control. I should have done this for you from the start. Forgive me, my love."

***

"How are you feeling, my love?" was Marco's morning greeting when he watched Liz wake up.

"Last night was intense. I apologize, Don, if I stepped out of line."

"If it were any other woman, they wouldn't have gotten away with such disrespect. But none would dare to reprimand or punish you when it's my job to do so."

Liz stopped stretching and turned to face him. "And are you going to punish me?" she asked and then bit her lip.

"All day, il Mia amore."

Grabbing both her arms he pulled her to his chest and kissed her hard. Liz opened her mouth and allowed his kiss to deepen. Then he pulled away.

"Stand up in front of the bed and take your clothes off slowly," he commanded.

Liz walked around the bed and stood in front of him and then lowered the straps, of her nightgown, pulling them off her shoulder as she watched Marco sitting against the headboard, grabbing, and stroking the growing tent until his cock was so restrained. He gasped as he quickly undid the zip of his trousers and freed the monster.

Liz was now standing in nothing but a white lace thong.

"Come here," Marco ordered.

She walked over to him and watched him put a pillow on the floor.

"Kneel," Marco said, and she did as she was told. Her mouth-watering at the sight of his stiff and leaking cock.

She bent her head and waited for his command he nodded. Then she pulled her tongue out and licked the tip of his cock, the cum salty and sweet-tasting, like the pineapple tart they had eaten the night before.

She looked up at him and smiled as he winked and smiled back. Then Liz devoured him. Taking as much of him as she could fit in her mouth and down her throat.

Liz listened proudly as he groaned and threw Italian words out as she continued to suck and lick until he pulled out of her mouth and told her to close her eyes. She felt the shooting warm cum cover her eyes, cheeks, and mouth. He yelled out her name as he painted her face with his seed.

"Stay there, don't move," Marco said panting, as he came down from his high.

Liz waited and then felt a warm cloth covering her face, as Marco washed off his cum.

"You can open your eyes now," he said. "You looked so fucking beautiful with my cum all over your face. I'm guessing no one has done that before?"

Liz shook her head as he took her hand and pulled her off the pillow until she was standing in his arms again.

"You are breathtaking, Elizabeth, my queen. You belong to me, and God help anyone who looks or touches you the wrong way. What happened will never happen again. You showed that you're feisty and worthy of respect"

Liz giggled. "Yeah, certainly tougher than Alisha thought."

"You handled yourself with dignity and showed your power. I couldn't be prouder. The men accept you as their queen, my wife."

Marco bent down and kissed her lips gently. "Il Mia amore," he whispered in her ear, before taking her hand and leading her back to the bed.

CHAPTER TWELVE
THE END OF THE DREAM

After they had finished their rounds of lovemaking, they had a shower and then dressed for the day. Liz got the impression that Marco was nervous. He was very quiet, and it seemed like he was going to say something to her, but then chickened out.

"So, Mia Caro. Have you thought about when you would like to get married?"

"I would marry you tomorrow if we could arrange it so fast," she answered hopefully.

He turned and pulled her body into his and kissed her softly. "Do you think you can have everything arranged in a week?" he asked.

Her eyes opened wide, to see if it was a jest. He nodded.

She smiled up at him. "I think the sooner I take your name, the better."

"Perfect." He said as he picked her up and spun her around and she squealed in delight.

"I will arrange for you to talk with a wedding planner and I'm sure the rest of the ladies in the house will be all too happy to help you."

"Not all." Liz sighed.

"Don't worry about Sara. She's visiting family for a few weeks."

"Oh, that's a relief. Wedding planning is stressful enough without adding Sara in the mix."

Marco hugged her and then pulled away so he could see her face.

"No, my love I don't want you to get stressed about this. Maybe the girls can handle all the arrangements."

Liz stepped back and shook her head.

"Marco. All little girls dream of their wedding day: the dress, the flowers, their husband. I didn't have any say in the arrangements for my wedding to Yuri. My mother took over everything and my opinion wasn't asked or wanted. Please don't take this away from me for a second time."

Marco wiped away the tear that dropped down her face. "Oh, my love. You will have the wedding of your dreams. I promise you. Anything you want. This will be the wedding you dreamed of as a little girl."

Liz grinned and jumped into his arms. "Thank you." She whispered in his ear. He patted her bum and she jumped back down.

"Now I must leave, I have a business to attend to. Please don't leave this room. We will have many men around the mansion today who don't know of you and who you are to me. Also, don't go outside on the balcony."

"Marco. What's going on?"

"Nothing for you to worry about, my love. Enzo will be in later to talk to you about something. Please do as I ask?"

"Of course," Liz agreed.

"I'll send Maria up with some breakfast. Be good." He

kissed her on the head before leaving the room.

Only ten minutes later, there was a knock on the door and Liz opened it to find Maria standing outside with a tray in her hands. As Liz opened the door to let her in, she noticed the house was alive with activity. Men and servants were rushing around and there were three guards stationed outside her room. They nodded in her direction before Liz closed the door.

Maria put the tray down on the bed and waited for Liz to sit.

"What is going on out there?" Liz asked, not expecting an answer.

"Nothing for you to worry about, Donna. Please eat your breakfast."

"For some reason, I've lost my appetite." Liz folded her arms. "I know something's going down. I've seen the worry in the Don's eyes, although he tried to hide it. Are they here? Have they found me?"

"I don't know what to tell you, Donna"

There was a loud rap on the door and Enzo entered and gestured for Maria to leave, which she did in a hurry.

"I'm not stupid. I know something is going on."

"I never thought you were," Enzo answered and smiled. But it was tight and forced, Liz thought.

She huffed and then sat on the bed with her head down. When she lifted her head, she turned to him and said. "They have found me, haven't they?"

Enzo nodded. "The house has been compromised and we have to move you out as soon as possible. Maria will help you pack essentials. I assure you the safe house is stocked up with everything you need for your comfort and safety. We have armed guards surrounding the place. It's impregnable. So have no worries, Donna."

"I knew this would happen. It was only a matter of time. So how far is the safe house from here?"

"It is a two-hour drive. We will be going in a convoy of SUVs. They are bulletproof, and each car will have four armed guards."

"And Marco. Where will he be? Where will you be? You're both coming as well?" Liz asked. Her heart started racing and her hand became sweaty.

"Not directly. We have unfinished business, but we will be making the move as soon as we can. Please, don't worry. Every precaution had been taken. We have been ready for this for a while now. Donna – Liz are you alright?"

All Liz heard was muffled talking and then shouting. Her breath had caught in her throat, and she couldn't breathe. Then she felt someone sitting behind her and whispering in her ear, urging her to stay calm and follow his breathing. She did as she was told and eventually, she controlled her breathing, her chest no longer felt tight, but being exhausted she fell asleep in Marco's arms. She never heard the whispered conversation.

"She can't cope with this move, especially being without you. She'll need to be sedated." Enzo said.

"I think you're right. Call the doctor and get Maria up here to pack a suitcase."

"How do you think she's going to react when she finds out you're staying to fight?"

Liz woke up again to screeching tyres, gunfire and yelling.

CHAPTER THIRTEEN

THE START OF A NIGHTMARE

Liz knew from the sporadic gunfire, that they were under attack, but where the hell was, she? The last thing she remembered was being in Marco's arms. She laid on the back seat, alone. She couldn't move her body and her mind was foggy. She knew she had to get out of the car, but no matter how much she willed it, she couldn't move, couldn't call for help. She just lay there, helpless. Her heart started racing when the bullets stopped firing and the car door was flung open.

Her legs were suddenly grabbed, and she was pulled out of the car and fell facedown onto the hard ground.

"What's wrong with her?"

"They sedated her. But I got her to swallow a Rohypnol as well."

Even though he was speaking Russian, Liz recognised his voice. It was Nicolo.

"The date rape drug and sedated you say? So, she can't move, but she knows what's happening?"

"Supposedly. But I don't know how lucid she is. I don't know how much they gave her. It could be wearing off now."

"Get her on her knees. Hold her up and keep her mouth open. I'll give the Greek whore what she's been dying for."

"Hurry it up. We haven't got time for this. The police could come any time!" Nicolo said.

"Don't worry. You'll get your turn."

Liz was being pulled around and, her hair grabbed until she was facing the man's crotch. There was nothing she could do to prevent him from ramming his disgusting cock down her throat when three others held her in place. He forced her to gag and choke while everyone around cheered, watching, and encouraging him.

She couldn't understand why this was happening to her and there was someone she needed or should be there. Why was she alone? But her mind was too fogged up to think clearly. And her head hurt when she tried to force a memory. *Maybe Nicolo would have a change of heart and get me out of here* but that hope vanished when she heard him yell,

"Choke the whore!"

Liz felt a hand pressing against her throat restricting her breathing, in turn, it caused her throat to shrink and for his cock to be stimulated more by her throat squeezing him. She started feeling lightheaded and knew it wasn't the sedation. The guy was choking her to death while fucking her mouth.

Liz psyched herself up forced her jaw to close and teeth to bite down on his cock. She heard screaming and her mouth filled up with blood. She spat it out at whoever was in front of her. Among the screaming and yelling and panic, someone backhanded her, and the force threw her to the ground where her head bounced off the gravelled surface before knocking her out.

Liz woke up to her worst nightmare. She was lying on the back seats of a car as Nicolo was pulling down her pants and pushing her legs open.

"No!" She screamed and struggled to get out of his grip.

But one hand, held both of hers above her head while the other reached into his pants and pulled out his cock pushing it straight inside her, raw.

She screamed and tears ran down her face from the pain as he kept ramming his cock inside her, hard and fast.

She finally got her voice back and screamed at him. "Nicolo, please stop. Don't do this."

"He killed Diane, Alishia and my Sara, for you, an MI5 spy and a Greek whore. Did you know that he killed my wife because of you? So now it's payback time, bitch, and I want to see why Marco kept you around for so long and now I know. You're so fucking tight, but you like it hard and fast don't you slut."

"No, no," she screamed. "I'm sorry." She sobbed out. "Nicolo, I didn't know about Sara or Diane."

"Exactly. You don't know who Marco is. You've never seen the Don in action. He's a sadistic murderer who kills without thought or shame. Women, children, he slaughters whole families just to get his point across. And you were going to marry him. You, fucking whore. Yeah, you like that, don't you?"

His hand started rubbing her clit. While he kept pounding inside her. she soon felt the tightness in her stomach before the driver turned around and said.

"Hurry it up, we're nearly there!"

"Come on, you Greek slut, cum for me."

He rubbed her clit faster. But the pain of dry sex and the migraine she was suffering from, stopped her from having any other reaction to him apart from disgust. She felt his warm seed filling her up, then he removed himself and dressed while she turned her head and body away from him.

She sobbed and wished that Marco would save her. But then she remembered they had a fight of their own back at the mansion, but it must have been a trap. Tears fell as she prayed that Marco was okay, and they would make it in time to save her. It was just the driver and Nicolo, who was laughing at her, in the car. She wondered what had happened to Marco and Luca. They didn't seem the kind of mafia that would think twice about putting a bullet in an enemy's head. Liz knew she was in an impossible situation, and it was very unlikely she was going to come out of it alive

"Oh, Yuri is gonna have fun with you, bitch." Nicolo laughed. "You're gonna pay and I'm going to soak up every swish of the belt, slash of the knife and scream you make while your arse is being ripped apart. You're in for a fun time.

He laughed sadistically and all she could do was cry and hope for a quick death. Liz knew she was in a lot of trouble and prayed that Marco and the other Capos were okay, and they would live through the battle.

Her hair was pulled again, and she felt the cloth cover her mouth as she breathed in the sweet chemicals.

***

Liz woke groggily and her mind was foggy until she remembered what had happened and her blurred vision came clear again, and she saw where she was.

A four-walled cell greeted her. The stench of old blood, urine, and faeces, caused her to gag. And as she looked down at her bare legs, she realised she was naked. They had her wrists cuffed and chained to the wooden beams in the middle of the cell. Her arms had been stretched. Her legs too had been cuffed and chained tightly to the floor, spreading her legs out so her body was in a star position open for any physical or sexual attack.

***

Liz stopped counting the men who came inside the cell and raped and abused her body. Sometimes two at a time and her screams just spurred them on. She felt their fluids run down her legs, from both passages. The last thought Liz had before her body gave up was that Yuri allowed the multiple rapes, which means he didn't want her as a wife anymore, which also meant he would kill her after they had finished. She hoped it was sooner rather than later. Her reprieve didn't last long; she was woken as ice cold water was thrown in her face.

Her hair was grabbed, and her head forced up. The man himself was staring at her.

"How are you enjoying the accommodation? The room service is good, yes. Had your fill of cock yet, whore?"

Liz wanted to spit in his face, but she had no saliva, so she stared him in the eye and said, "You are a sick sadistic monster, and I can't wait until I get the opportunity to cut your heart out. Believe me, I will!"

Yuri laughed. "Argh, slut, I've always liked your fighting spirit. You will make a perfect pet once trained. It's good you speak our motherland's tongue; it will be easier for you to follow directions."

He turned his head to the side and ordered his men.

"Get her cleaned up and then brought to my study."

Turning back around to Liz, and still holding her head up by her hair he said.

"Lizzy, tonight I will allow you to rest. I'm sure your body is exhausted with all the cocks that fucked you today." He laughed. "But tomorrow we start your training after we have a little chat."

His smirk told her that there the chat was going to be more like an interrogation and that she was in for a lot of pain.

More ice-cold water was thrown at her and then two women with long yard brushes started scrubbing her body and laughed as she screamed at them to stop.

***

Marco was exhausted from the fight but came away with just a bullet in his shoulder and cuts and bruises.

Enzo had The King of the Greek mafia kneeling on the floor, hands tied behind his back. Knowing Marco wanted to probably prolong the torture of Liz's father he kept him alive but made sure he got a workout on his face.

There were casualties. Marco expected that, but the allies he had trusted came through and within minutes the Greeks were gunned down and the king was alive and waiting for his execution.

Jacob Mirsklavou lifted his head and laughed when he saw Marco walking into the room, surrounded by his Capos and the guards.

"You'll never find her." Jacob laughed.

"What is he talking about?" Enzo asked, looking at Marco.

"Ha! You don't even know. My darling daughter has probably been fucked to death by now."

Marco didn't allow Jacob to get another word in, he lifted the gun and shot him straight between the eyes. The King was dead and now only Liz remained from the family, making her the Queen of the Greek mafia.

"I can't get hold of Mario or Luca." Enzo closed his phone.

"What the fuck do you think happened?"

"I think that Russian bastard used the Greeks as cover whilst he ambushed and took my queen!"

***

Still naked but virtually clean of sperm and blood, Liz was unchained and dragged to the office where Yuri waited. Too exhausted in mind, body, and spirit, she didn't care where they took her or what happened to her next. So, it was a surprise when she was pulled over and forced to lie on a large soft cushion, next to a warming fire. Her eyes closed as soon as the warmth and comfort took over her body. She felt something go around her neck, her hair was pushed off her face and her head was gently patted as words were whispered into her ear.

"Rest now, my kitten, you have a long day ahead of you tomorrow. Don't worry my cock won't go anywhere near your dirty used pussy. You had your chance. But we're still going to have a lot of fun together and I can't wait to play with you. Sleep now, Kitten. "

Liz woke to someone yelling and screaming at her and then her hair was pulled until she fell off the cushion and to the cold wooden floor.

"Get on your knees now, whore!"

Yuri yelled at her and then spat in her face. She moved her sore and aching body until she was kneeling in front of him. His cock standing swollen in front of her face. Knowing what he wanted her to do, she opened her mouth and took him in. She felt him stroking her head as he said,

"Good kitten, you know exactly what your master wants. Maybe you won't be as hard to train as I thought. This will be the first thing you do every morning. You come and drink your master's milk, like a good kitten. Yes, that's it. Take it all in, my pet. Open your throat…. Umm, that's good. So good. Who taught you how to suck cock so good? Was it that Italians? Yeah, I bet it was. I bet you were on your knees most of the time and you fucking love it. Don't you?"

Liz face whipped to the left as Yuri bought his hand across her cheek.

"Did you choke on the Italian bastard's cock like this?"

Liz felt her nose being pinched as he held on tightly to her hair and pushed the back of her head until her nose was touching his pubes. There was no way for her to get air in and she struggled in his solid grip until she felt his warm salty cum drip down her throat, then he threw her off him.

She choked out his cum as she gasped for air, which made him red with rage.

"I give you the honour of my cum and you spit it on the floor. Lick it up, my pet. Now!"

Pushing her face into the puddle of cum with his foot, Liz slowly pulled out her tongue and licked the cold slime off the floor. She gagged, but she knew she had to keep it inside. She didn't hear Yuri taking off his belt. But she heard the belt swishing in the air before it came down on her naked skin over and over again. She screamed in pain, in between trying to lick up all the mess.

"Maybe that will teach you to treasure the food your master gives you and swallow it next time, Kitten. Now stand up. Go with these two men and don't try anything, they have been given clear instructions of what's to happen, if you do. I will be down soon to have a little chat with you."

She never did anything to cause them problems and just followed in between them until she was taken into a cold room that was decorated in silver metal surfaces and surrounded by metal draws, but her compliance didn't stop the guards from raping her and slapping her around before she was lifted and strapped to a cold metal table. Liz realised she was in a morgue.

The two guards stood with their arms folded. Heads looking straight ahead and stood like statues.

"What happened here?"

Was the first thing Yuri asked when he came inside and saw the blood dripping from her mouth.

"She tried to run." One of the guards said and shrugged while the other winked and smiled at his friend.

Which didn't go unnoticed by Yuri. Turning to face them he glared. "I doubt that very much. She's been sedated. She wouldn't have been able to skip past you, let alone run. Leave, you're both dismissed."

The guards ran out of the room, as Yuri took a cloth and wiped away the blood on her lips.

"Oh, my dear, pet. What am I going to do with you? Kitten, I'm going to ask you some questions and I know you're going to tell me the truth as you have a truth serum running through your blood."

Yuri caressed her head as he stared at her naked body before looking back at her face, and then asking his first question.

"Do you love me?"

"No" she answered immediately.

Liz felt a shock of electricity, flow through her body. She reached up to her neck, where the shock originated from and felt a thick metal collar. Remembering something being put on her neck that night but she'd been too out of it.

"Well, at least we know the drug and the shock collar is working. Shh, it is okay, my pet!"

He stroked her head again as tears escaped from her eyes.

"Although there is no longer a wedding. How were the preparations going?"

Liz started talking rapidly, although hyped up. The words just flowed out and she couldn't stop them coming out of her mouth.

"Mama had everything arranged. The bouquet was green and cream, and the cake was white with green vine leaves. I was worried about the cake being able to travel well, but the baker said there was no problem."

He smiled down at her

"That's good, Kitten. Now, tell me what happened on Thursday the 11th of March?"

Liz tried to recall the date and her eyes lit up as she grabbed onto Yuri's hands and told him about trying on all the hideous dresses, but then she found the one.

"Oh, Yuri, you would have loved it!" She gushed.

"It was almost all lace and very silhouette. It had a long sleeve and a high neck, but it showed off my figure."

"Yes, yes," Yuri barked impatiently.

"What happened next?"

"We were celebrating after finding the dress and drinking champagne..."

Yuri watched her smile falter and the light going out of her eyes.

"Then I started feeling dizzy and I remember falling off the pedestal I was standing on and I don't remember what happened after that. Oh, there was an explosion, I think. I was kidnapped. The Italians. They…"

She started to cry. and told him of the torture they put her through.

"They never raped me like you allowed Nicolo and your men to do."

"Nicolo?"

"Yes, he raped me in the car as they were bringing me to you. He doesn't like me much. He and his wife, Sara, didn't want me there and they wanted to get rid of me. So, he hurt me badly and he killed my mother and cousins. I think he doesn't like the Greeks. He will do anything to get rid of me. He is Marco's brother, but he hated me from the start."

"So, you were never raped whilst in the hands of the Italian? Did Marco hurt you?"

"No, I wasn't. They don't do that to females, even prisoners. They have too much respect for women. Marco was never a part of my torture, but he could be mean and choked me once."

"Why did you agree to marry him. When you were my betrothed?"

He watched Liz's pupils dilate and then stare unmoving. He slapped her cheek.

"Hey, Elizabeth, stay with me."

"I don't feel so good. My heart wants to jump out of my chest."

"Why did you agree to marry him?" Yuri asked again and then called out.

"Doctor in here now."

"Marriage of convenience." She answered. "For the same reason, you wanted to marry me. He wanted Greece," She slurred and then her eyes closed, and her head fell to the side.

The door opened at the same time Yuri was checking for a pulse.

"She's not breathing," Yuri yelled to the doctor.

"This is who you wanted the truth serum for? I didn't know you were going to use it on a woman and one who looks like she's barely hanging on."

He put a stethoscope to her chest and then turned around and looked at Yuri with a grave expression. "Her heart has stopped. She's dead. The serum is used by the KGB for getting answers and then it speeds up the heart rate and causes the heart to stop. I didn't know that you wanted the serum just to get the truth out of someone, or that your prisoner was female."

"She's not a prisoner."

"You could have fooled me from what I've heard she's had done to her."

"It was a mistake," Yuri mumbled. And then turned and grabbed the doctor's shirt.

"You get her heart beating again, or this bullet has your name on it. She's worth more alive than dead!" Yuri pulled out his gun and held it to the doctor's head.

The doctor gulped and then took the defibrillator, started it up, made sure everything was clear and then shocked her. Only as he did, the shock collar short-circuited and flames came out of the machine, burning the skin off her neck until they had extinguished the flames and broken the collar off.

"Why the hell didn't you mention that before I sent 300 volts of electricity through her!"

Yuri was pacing the room. "He lied to me. I will kill him." He mumbled to himself. And then turned to the doctor.

"Did it work? Is she breathing?"

The doctor examined her and shook his head and then started CPR. After two rounds, he used the defibrillator again. Both knew that the longer her heart wasn't beating, the less chance there was to bring her back. The doctor charged it up again, put the paddles on her chest and pressed the button. He then took his stethoscope and listened carefully.

He sighed in relief.

"I can hear a heartbeat, but it's faint. We need to get her transferred to a hospital as soon as possible. But it's not a secure location.

"Don't you worry about that; I will have my men surrounding the place. No one will go in or out. You just worry about keeping her alive or I will burn your house down with your family still inside after I've let my men rape your wife and daughter. Do you hear me, doctor? This is your fault. Now fix it, or I will fix you permanently. I have plans for her and you better not have ruined them.

CHAPTER FOURTEEN
THE TRAITOR

Back at the mansion, three men were watching a screen that showed a map and a blinking red dot.

"What the hell just happened? Where has the signal gone?" Marco yelled.

"They either found the implant and destroyed it..." Stefano said, and then swallowed.

"Or?" Enzo urged.

Stefano looked up at Marco. "Or it short-circuited?"

"Meaning it was fried and only electricity could have done that."

Marco grabbed a hold of his hair and growled.

The men glanced at Marco

"I'm sorry, Boss." Stefano quietly said.

"Don't tell me you're fucking sorry. Find out what's around there, before we lost her signal. Find out who owns those warehouses. Enzo, gather the men and our allies, those that are fit to fight. This war has just begun. I'm going to slaughter that Russian bastard."

Marco left the room as he barked orders to the men standing and sitting inside the house waiting for news.

"Those of you that are injured and can no longer fight, I thank you for your service. Go home and rest, you will be rewarded. The rest of you, eat and rest, our fight is not over. And once we have their location, we're getting back our queen."

Cheers erupted, but Marco didn't feel it was right to join in. Until he had Liz back in his arms, he couldn't let any emotion get in the way. Strolling in the kitchen he took a handful of sandwiches from a plate and a soda from the fridge.

"Thank you."

The kitchen staff acknowledged his gratefulness and continued to make sandwiches for the hungry men.

Marco walked out into the back patio and sat down as he munched on the sandwiches, not that he was hungry or tasted anything, but he knew he needed to keep his strength up.

"Don, let me take a look at your shoulder." The doctor said as she walked towards him.

"It's merely a scratch. Go and help someone who needs it."

"You need it," she argued.

"I can't afford to have my shoulder strapped. I need to be able to use all my limbs for the fight that is about to go down."

Not deterred, she said. "Well, at least let me take the bullet out and clean it up, so it doesn't get infected."

Marco glared at her. The doctor stepped back and held her hands up, "No strap, I promise."

"And no anaesthetic. I need to be able to feel it," he barked.

"Very well." She nodded and then opened her surgical bag.

He paid no attention to her, apart from wincing when she dug inside his flesh to find the bullet. The rest of the time, his mind was on Liz. What was being done to her? *Stay strong, my darling, I'm coming for you.*

Enzo then came rushing outside. "We've found them." He grinned and then made a face as he saw the gaping hole in his Don's shoulder.

"Get the men ready to leave." Marco gritted his teeth. "Sew this up quickly"

"Yes, Don." She pulled out a sterile surgical set. Laying it on the table she opened it up and got to work. The doctor worked fast, not wanting to face the Don's wrath.

"Tell me, doc. How much electricity would be needed to short circuit the tracking device you have in you?"

Every member of his mafia had a tracking device. Marco wanted to know where everyone was at any time.

The doctor frowned before answering. "To short circuit one of these bad boys," she pointed to the back of her neck. "It would take at least 5000 volts."

"Enough to kill someone?" Marco asked quietly.

"Maybe. It depends on the current situation and if that person was close to metal or another source of electricity. Why are you asking?" She covered her mouth with her hands. "No, you don't think…"

"Look, just do your job here and be ready, because I have a feeling Liz is gonna need you. And Lucinda, set everything up in my room."

"Si, Don," she answered, and bowed her head as Marco rushed past and entered the house.

***

"Boss, I don't like this. Where are the guards? Where are the cars? It could be a trap," Stefano said.

"Why are we here at this warehouse?" Marco asked him.

"Because it's owned by Yuri's Russian cousin," Enzo answered instead.

"Exactly, so we are at the right place. So, stop the fucking whining and let's take a closer look, yes?"

Noticing the cameras aimed at the warehouse door, Marco signalled for Stefano to cut the feed and for another one of his men to climb the roof and use the heat-seeking cameras. Quickly, Marco was told the feed was cut and that there was only one person in the building, and they were on the floor not moving.

"Let's go.

Marco ordered the men to open the door. Hunching down quickly, they touched the door, and Enzo stepped in first. Once Marco was given the all-clear he entered and ran towards the office where the injured person was.

Before he stepped through, Enzo whispered to Marco that it was his brother, Nicolo and that someone had chopped off his dick. He'd lost a lot of blood and was close to death.

Marco crouched down to his brother, and slapped his face, "Nicolo – Nicolo wake up."

Nicolo opened his eyes. Marco knew from the glazed that covered his eyes, that Nicolo's vision would be impaired.

"Brother!" Nicolo croaked out and coughed up blood.

Marco took the front of Nicolo's shirt and pulled him up to his face. "Where is she?" He yelled.

"Of course, always the princess everyone wants. Well, we all had her." Nicolo laughed and coughed up more blood.

"What are you talking about?" Marco asked.

Nicolo, took some breaths, still laughing through blood-stained teeth. He said, "When I told Yuri what a whore she was, he handed her over to his guards to do what they wanted with her. And they did, we all did, and I under-stand why you wanted her so bad, her cunt was so tight. Not now though."

Marco stepped away, throwing Nicolo's body away in disgust.

"Where is she?" Marco growled and pulled his gun out aiming it at his brother's head.

"Even now she has you Dons wrapped around her fin-ger. You're just weak pansy pussies. First you, then Yuri, and you still want her back after I've just told you every hole was used and abused for fucking days. I relished her screams." Marco fired the gun into Nicolo's leg.

"Where is Elizabeth?" Marco asked again.

"You're too late. She's dead. Her heart gave out while she was being interrogated. But Yuri found out I exagger-ated a small touch and wasn't happy with me or himself. I think she's won him over, but by then it was too late."

Nicolo continued laughing until Enzo, Marco and Stefano opened fire and riddled his body with bullets.

"Do you believe him?" Enzo asked.

"I need to see her body to believe she's gone. Until then, I will search and burn this town to the ground."

Everyone around him started searching for information and evidence, to find Elizabeth.

"Boss. I think I've got something." Enzo seemed triumphant.

"The local hospital is not picking up the telephone, which I thought was a bit strange, so I sent Dimitri to check it out. It's shut down tight, with guards standing outside."

"Send everyone there to storm the place. If anyone refuses entry, shoot them. No one has the right to close one of my hospitals down. I know she's there and that means she's alive."

Marco stepped on the gas and drove like a maniac determined to be the first to arrive and shoot some Russian bastards. He couldn't get the image of them touching, raping, and torturing her out of his mind. He would make everyone pay, he vowed.

CHAPTER FIFTEEN

PAYING THE PRICE

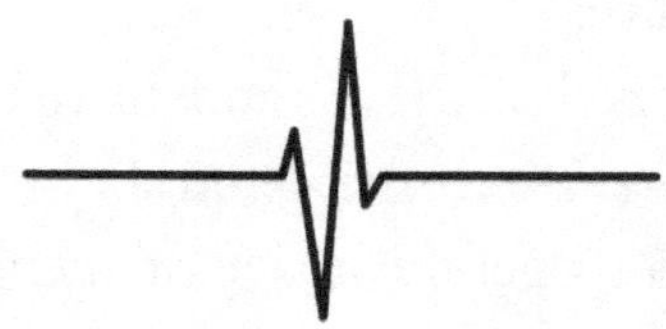

Yuri was pacing the corridor as he waited for news on Elizabeth's condition. Why had he listened to that lying Italian scum? He'd just given her up to his men, who violated and tortured her, all because he'd been told she was a whore and sucking the dicks of the Italian mafia. It wasn't until the serum worked, that he found out the truth. But then it was too late. He'd thrown his bride to his dogs and then injected her with a lethal drug. He killed her. He killed off any chance he had of owning her.

Whilst Yuri was feeling pissed about the thought of losing his pet, he didn't hear the main doors to the hospital slide open. He didn't see Marco walking towards him with a gun held out. It wasn't until he felt the bullet rip through his chest, that he looked up and saw Marco standing in front of him firing the gun again.

Marco stood over Yuri's body that was bleeding out.

His gun aimed at Yuri's head.

"She should have been mine," Yuri said, spitting out blood.

"Never!" Marco yelled as his finger pressed down on the trigger, shooting the Russian Mafia boss in the head.

Two doctors came running around the corner and when they saw the scene and recognised Marco. They lifted their arms in surrender.

"Forgive us, Mr Lucianno. We had no choice but to do as he said. He shot dead five of our residents."

Marco glared at them, although his finger was itching to pull the trigger again, he needed to find Elizabeth.

"Where is my wife?"

"Please, Don Lucianno, this way. A Russian surgeon is working on her."

"What! You find me, Italian surgeons, now! You show me where that Russian pig is."

Marco ran with the other doctor as he shouted orders to Enzo and his men. He ran down the empty corridor following the doctor.

"How is she? What's her condition?"

The doctor stopped outside a door and rapped on it. As two other surgeons came running up, breathlessly. Still wearing masks and bloodied gloves, they bowed to Marco. The surgery door opened and the man in a green gown stared daggers at the three doctors two the right, and then when he turned and noticed Marco, his eyebrows lifted in surprise.

Marco dragged him away from the door as the two doctors and surgeons ran inside.

"How is my wife? Is she still alive?" Marco had him

pinned to the wall and spoke very calmly to the Russian.

The surgeon nodded and that gave Marco hope.

"Her heart was weakened by poison of some sort. We are still running tests. When the electricity travelled through her body, it stopped her heart. We have stabilised her, but she will need a heart transplant as soon as we can find a suitable match. We have applied a skin graft to her neck to cover the extensive burn and..." He stopped and bent his head

"Tell me everything." Marco gritted his teeth and the hold of the doctor's lab coat gripped tighter.

"There was extensive tearing of her back passage and her vagina. She had a lot of bleeding and needed internal stitching to repair the damage."

Marco closed his eyes for a moment and then looked back at the surgeon and asked the question.

"How sick is my wife? What are her chances?"

Enzo then appeared and stood beside his Don, not surprised when he saw Marco's eyes shining with water.

"She's in critical condition. Her heart could give out again at any time."

"Again?" Enzo said. "How many times has this happened?"

The Russian glanced at both Italians before stating she had flat-lined three times while on the operating table.

"Your wife is in a coma. But this is good news as it allows her body time to heal while we look for a suitable match for her."

"And how long does she have if we can't find a donor?"

"Her heart has been weakened so much; it could give out anytime."

"What is her match? Tell me all the specifics and I'll get you a heart." Enzo asked.

The doctor explained everything, as Enzo wrote it all down and then ran out of the hospital entrance.

"Thank you for answering my questions." Then Marco shot five bullets into the man's stomach, before letting go of his collar and watching him fall to the floor.

One of the surgeons came out to see what happened.

"Can I see her?" Marco asked him.

"Let me get her cleaned up and moved to a private room first. Believe me, you don't want to go inside right now. Ten minutes. Okay, Don Lucianno?"

"I will come and get you when she is settled." The surgeon returned to the operating room.

***

Only two days later, Enzo handed a heart to the surgeon, that matched Liz's needs. It was wrapped up and laid on ice in an official medical box. Although the doctor raised his eyebrows, he never questioned where the heart came from. The sooner he could get the woman out of intensive care, the more he'd be able to breathe. Ever since she'd been admitted, he felt a weight on his shoulder and that weight was named Don Marco Lucianno.

Marco grabbed Enzo and pulled him to his chest and held him tight.

"Thank you, brother. You have lived up to your station and the oath you gave us. You'll be rewarded well."

"Bah!" Enzo disagreed. "I did this out of love and respect to my King and Queen. I expect nothing in return and will not take a dime. But thank you, brother, for your generous offer."

The heart transplant took ages and many of Marco's men came to pay their respect and hopefully hear some good news.

Marco was going crazy. The longer he waited, the more anxious he became.

"What's taking him so long? It should have been over by now unless there were complications."

Marco made the sign of the cross then kissed his golden cross pendant, which hung around his neck.

It's been twelve hours. Please let this operation be successful and bring back my Elizabeth to me. She doesn't deserve what's happened to her. She is an innocent soul and none of this would have happened if we'd never met. But then again, it was fated that we'd meet, and I thank you, Lord, for bringing her to me. Liz is my soulmate. I know I have only two choices. But I can't live without her so I know what I must do. Watch over my angel, Lord. Keep her safe and bring her back to me.

Marco got up from his chair and stood beside Enzo.

"Let us walk. Stefano, call me if you hear anything."

"Will do, Boss."

"How are you doing?" Enzo asked Marco, as they started to walk down an empty corridor.

"I need to talk with you about something serious. Let's go to the garden, where our conversation won't be heard."

Enzo nodded and followed Marco.

"Liz is as pure and innocent as they come. I should never have taken her, I should never have had her interrogated and tortured, especially given her background. She should have been treated like a queen from the start. Alas, that is the past and I can do nothing to change that. Knowing what the bastard Russian did to her, passing her around like a whore to be raped and abused, I don't know if I can forgive myself. Again, this is on me."

Enzo tried to interrupt but Marco held up his hand to silence him.

"Yes, it's on me as Nicolo was my brother and I knew from the start his hate for the Greeks. I should never have allowed either of them anywhere near her. And killing Sara was the last thing that broke Nicolo. However, I was bound by mafia law as she broke the Omerta and confessed to being a rat. We had no choice but to follow our law. I should have kept a closer watch on Nicolo. Maybe then I would have found evidence that he was playing both sides. My gut tells me that if Nicolo hadn't told Yuri those disgusting lies about Liz, she wouldn't have been so badly beaten and abused."

Marco turned to face Enzo.

"She's been through enough. I can't allow anyone to go near her again. That leaves me with two options, and I think you know which one I have chosen?"

Enzo nodded. "You're ready to step down as king and give up everything you've worked hard for?"

"I never considered that making Liz my queen would put an even bigger target on her. All I cared about was getting rid of the Greeks and the Russians and getting her mentally stable again. But now I realise she needs to be away from the toxic lifestyle, away from any threat, if she's going to get over the abuse she's suffered."

"But Boss. The only way you can walk away from the mafia is in a body bag?"

Marco grinned when he saw the confusion on Enzo's face.

"What's the plan, Boss?"

"From now on, you are the boss. Enzo, I entrust my mafia into your capable hands. However, appearances need to be kept, so I will play my part right to the end, Don Enzo Lucianno." Marco bowed his head.

"So, how are you thinking of doing this?" Enzo asked.

"I think we deserve to go out in spectacular style. Once Elizabeth has recovered, we will be going on a trip on my private jet. There will be an emergency and the plane will dive and crash into whatever is below us. All that will remain is our charred bodies. Only dental records will identify that we have both been killed in an unfortunate accident."

Marco smiled, as did Enzo.

Enzo patted Marco's shoulder. "And I have the perfect place for both of you to live without being discovered or in danger."

The two continued discussing plans until Marco's phone rang.

***

The surgery was a success, but Liz was still in a coma. The doctors were certain she would come out of it quickly, but weeks passed and there was no change. Marco had her moved to the house at night, secretly. No one was to know about what happened or about the surgery she had. Enzo and his men made sure anyone connected who wasn't family or an ally was eliminated. As far as anyone knew, she was healthy.

And that was the curious part. Liz was healthy again.

"She's just sleeping now," Lucinda told Marco. "But it's not to heal her body as that's healed remarkably quickly. I think she's taking this time to heal her mind. After everything that happened, she will wake up when she's ready."

"Do you think she hears me when I talk to her?" Marco asked.

"I'm sure she's heard every word you've said." Lucinda smiled.

"I want her to know that she's safe, that she's with me and that Yuri, her father, everyone who targeted her, are now dead."

"If that's what you've told her, then I believe she knows."

Marco laid his head down on the side of the bed and sighed. "Then why isn't she waking up?"

"Don – sorry – Marco." Lucinda bit her lip.

Even though she worked for the new Don of the Italian mafia, Enzo wouldn't allow her to leave until Liz was up, walking and 100% well, no matter how long it took. Lucinda had been ordered to stay with them, and who was she to argue with the luxury life she was now living?

Marco smiled at her slip up.

Lucinda touched his shoulder gently. "Just be patient. Keep talking to her and bring her around."

CHAPTER SIXTEEN
New Beginnings

Two weeks later, Marco saw Liz's finger move. He yelled for Lucinda.

After a quick examination, Lucinda was excited to tell Marco that she was waking, but it would be slow.

She touched his shoulder gently.

"You need to know what you'll be facing once she is awake."

"What do you mean?"

"Well, first there's her mental state. We have an idea of what went on, but we don't know everything and until she's ready to talk, she will be closed off, depressed and possibly suicidal. She will need support and love, but if she pushes you away, Marco, don't take it personally. It's just one of the stages she has to go through before acceptance. And then there's her physical being. Yes, she's healthy and all her organs are working well, but she hasn't eaten real food for over a month. She hasn't walked or used any of her limbs. She will need slow rehabilitation. She may never be the Liz you knew."

"Yes, she will," Marco argued. "She's too strong to let

those bastards win. I'll have my Liz back and I will do everything I need to get her back."

"These are just the worst-case scenarios – I just wanted to prepare you. I will go tell the chef to make a soup. Talk to her, convince her to open her eyes. I'm certain she's ready to see you again."

Marco waited until the doctor left the room, before taking hold of Liz's hand, he kissed it gently before saying, "My darling, I know you can hear me. It's your fiancé. We're supposed to be getting married, remember? It's just you and me. No one is here, so please open your beautiful eyes. You've slept long enough. It's time to come back to me."

But instead of her opening her eyes, he felt her squeezing his hand.

"Liz, my darling. Open your eyes and look at me, honey."

"So, when is the date?" she managed to half-whisper and croak out.

Marco stood up and kissed her lips as tears ran down his face. Liz slowly lifted her arm, opened her eyes, and touched his cheek wiping away his tears before the arm fell limply to the bed.

"How long have I been asleep for this time?" she whispered.

"A while. Let me call the doctor to check you over." Marco went to walk away when Liz grabbed his arm.

"I'm perfectly well, although I could do with a drink of water. My mouth feels like sandpaper."

"Of course." Marco went over to the counter and poured a glass of water.

He rushed back and watched her gulped it down eagerly,

and he cursed himself for not bringing the bottle over with him. Reaching over the top of the bed, he pressed a button.

"So, is it true?" Liz asked him.

"Is what true, my love?"

"That you gave up everything just so you could protect me?"

Marco gulped. "Yes, but I did for selfish reasons as well. So, you did hear me talking to you?"

"Not all the time. Some days you were clear and other times you mumbled words that meant nothing to me. But I've been fighting to get back to you."

"Oh, my darling." Marco scooped her up in his arms and hugged her, not as tight as he wanted.

"What's holding you back?"

Before Marco could rain down kisses on her, Lucinda came in and checked her over,

"Well, I'm happy to say, you're doing really well, especially after having such a major operation. You're a star patient." Lucinda smiled, before leaving them both alone.

Marco then took Liz in his arms and walked out onto the balcony. She gasped at the sight before her: aquamarine water, white sandy beach, and total peace, with no one around.

"Where are we?" she asked, still astonished at the view.

"This is our island. Our place. Enzo bought it for us as a wedding present. Only Lucinda, Enzo and Stefano know where we are."

"Umm, Marco, did we get married and I didn't know?"

He laughed and it was a rare sound that Liz hoped she would hear again.

"No, Mia Caro. That is to come when you are well. Just

know we are safe. No one is searching for us. Everyone else believes we are dead."

Liz pointed to a chair on the balcony, and Marco gently sat her down and then went back inside and put a blanket over her shoulders.

"How did you do it?" Liz took the glass of fruit juice and pain pills from Marco's hands.

"A plane crash. A complete random accident. Two charred bodies were identified only by dental records. It was a costly way to go." He mused.

"Damn shame." Liz winked and pulled Marco's shirt down so she could kiss him.

"We had a joint service. We were very popular and had many of the mafia families pay their respect."

"So, Enzo is the Don now?

"Yes. After our untimely demise, he inherited the title and as the Greek mafia was yours by right, so he's taken over that as well. Stefano does most of the work over there now. Don't worry, he has plenty of help and allies. He wanted to do this for you."

"What happened to Nicolo? You know he was playing both sides?"

Marco closed his eyes. He knew the question would eventually come up.

"We found him in the warehouse."

"We?" Liz asked as her heart started racing.

"Enzo, Stefano and I found Nicolo. Yuri had cut off his… well, he was bleeding out and wouldn't last the night, but he confessed everything before we filled him with bullets."

"You know what they did to me?" Liz couldn't face him.

"Only the three of us and Lucinda know. Everyone else was silenced, either paid off or killed." He squeezed her shoulder. "Lucinda and I are both here if ever you feel the need to talk about what happened. No rush. No pressure."

Liz had to ask. "And Yuri?"

"I put a gun to his head and ended him."

"You know he wanted me as a pet. He started training me and called me Kitten until he drugged me with a deadly truth serum, and everything just faded to black after that."

Marco filled in the blanks, leaving out unnecessary details. They sat together watching the sunset, wrapped in the blanket holding each other.

***

Both the doctor and Marco were surprised by her mental state, especially after what she'd been through. Apart from some night terrors, her spirit was upbeat. It was the rehabilitation that was taking its toll on her as well as Marco. All they could do was kiss and embrace one another, some foreplay, but it just wasn't enough. Finally, after a month, the doctor gave them the all-clear and Marco planned a special evening for them.

Liz dressed in the long, white maxi dress that had been laid on the bed and put on the beaded sandals that were placed on the floor. She then moved to the mirror and plaited the side of her hair before putting a halo of white flowers woven together by green foliage, on the top of her head. Liz didn't bother with makeup or perfume. There was no one to impress now and she knew Marco favoured the natural look. Although as a Donna to a mafia, she always had to appear perfect, her makeup flawless and her designer clothes to be new and crease-free, now she could live without rules and expectations.

Liz twirled the skirt whilst staring at her bohemian, effortless look. There was a tap on the door and Liz turned as she called, "Come in."

Lucinda peeked her head around the corner and then opened the door wide walked in and took both of Liz's hands.

"You are beautiful my dear. He's waiting for you on the beach, follow the roses." She smiled and winked before leaving the room.

"Lucinda," Liz called out. "I'm so happy you have decided to stay with us. I love your company."

Lucinda smiled. "Miss out on living in paradise for the rest of my life. Not a chance. Oh, and if you ever travel over to the mainland and see the local talent, that's just another reason for me to stay." Lucinda winked, before leaving and closing the door behind her.

Liz turned to the mirror one last time, played with her hair, took a deep breath, and then slid open the patio window and started walking down the cobbled path that was littered with white rose petals. The fragrance was intoxicating, and her heart raced in nervous anticipation. As soon as the beach came into sight, she stopped walking and covered her mouth with a gasp. The beach was lit up with flaming torches. The most beautiful, canopied bed covered with silk cushions and open net curtains sat on the beach as if it belonged there. But the sight that took her breath away was Marco in his white shirt and black trousers standing beside a laden dinner table. One hand was holding the back of a silver chair, the other hand reached out for her to take.

Liz ran to where he stood and threw herself onto him. Hugging him tightly, Marco whispered "You are stunning, Mia Caro. Do you know how much I love you?"

"I think I have an idea," she giggled.

No matter how good the five-class cuisine was, neither was hungry, at least not for food. They picked at their grilled fish, not saying a word, staring at each other, sipping full-bodied red wine. Finally, Marco spoke.

"That's enough. It's obvious we're going to have to work up an appetite before we can eat."

"Oh, and what did you have in mind?" She winked.

"How about an evening dip in the ocean?" Marco suggested.

"But I haven't got a swimsuit," Liz said and twirled her hair around her finger, quite happy to play his game.

"Stand up." Marco used his dominant voice and Liz stood up and waited for him.

Standing in front of her, he gently pulled each strap of her dress off her shoulders and watched as it fell onto the sand. Leaving Liz standing naked in front of him.

"Oh, mio Dio. Sei una dea."

(Oh, my God. You are a goddess.)

Liz giggled and started to run down the beach to the water, whilst Marco followed ripping off his clothes as he chased after her.

Liz stood frozen in the warm, black coloured water, staring at the full moon. It appeared so big, so close that if she reached out her hand, she could touch it.

"It's mesmerizing, just like you," Marco whispered, and taking her shoulders turned her around to face him.

He leant down and kissed her soft lips, but Liz had

hungered for him for what seemed like forever. She pulled him by the neck and deepened the kiss. Their tongues fought until they each playfully tasted one another. Tasting the wine made them want more, and they devoured each other's mouths until they had to stop to take a breath. Liz panted as Marco bent down and kissed her nipples before grabbing her and pulling her up until her legs were around his waist and her arms around his neck. She felt his hard cock positioned right next to her entrance, which was tingling in anticipation. When his lips slammed into hers, she felt his cock push inside and it had been so long, there was pain, as he stretched her out.

Marco groaned as he slowly pushed his way in.

"Are you, okay?" he asked, and she loved him for it.

Raising her body, she slammed down onto him. Pushing his cock deep inside her. She cried out in ecstasy as they both moved their bodies in sync, pounding into one another. Panting, splashing of water and loud moans were all that could be heard before Liz felt her orgasm exploding and screamed out profanities. Her clenching caused Marco to cum, and he filled her up as they both hung onto each other tightly while they came down from their high.

As she climbed down from his waist and hugged him, she realised that they hadn't used any protection.

"You, know I've been off the pill for a long time now. Can you get the morning after pill out here?" she asked doubtfully.

"No. And yes, I knew you've been off contraception."

"We could have just made a baby, you know."

He smiled. "I know. How do you feel about that?" He suddenly felt worried, like he'd made a big mistake.

Liz noticed his worried expression and her hand caressed his cheek. "We're getting married on this very beach in one week. Neither of us works and so the next step would be kids. It's not like it could happen the first time."

"So, would you mind practising more with me, Mrs Lucianno?"

"Umm, and it seems there's somewhere ideal, very close, where we can continue this conversation." She said, pulling him out of the water as they headed for the bed.

The food was forgotten and eaten cold for breakfast by a very exhausted but smiling couple.

ABOUT THE AUTHOR

Karina Kantas is a prolific author of 14 titles. Including the four-book, gritty MC thriller series, *Outlaw* and the exciting YA fantasy duology, *Illusional Reality*.

She also writes short stories and when her imagination is working overtime, she writes thought-provoking dark flash fiction.

There are many layers to Karina's writing style and voice, as you will see in her flash fiction collection, *Heads & Tales* and in *Undressed* she opens up more to her fans, giving them another glimpse into her warped mind.

When Karina isn't busy working on her next best-seller, she's a publicist, author manager and VA. She's also a radio host on the Artist First Radio Network and is YouTuber, podcaster, BookTuber and has won numerous International Film-Festival awards for her trailers and documentary. She is the host of the YouTube show, Behind The Pen.

Karina writes in the genres of fantasy, MC romance, Young Adult. sci-fi, horror, thrillers and comedy, romance, PNR, dystopian and erotica, dark mafia romance.

You can find her on Facebook and Twitter, where she loves hanging out with her readers.

Karina is happiest when listening to rock music or riding her motorbike.

Sign up to Karina Kantas mailing list to be the first for latest news, discounts, free books and regular contests.
http://eepurl.com/gSTe_9

For updated news, excerpts and latest publications come and say hi on her social media pages.

https://www.facebook.com/ExplosiveWriter

https://www.instagram.com/karinakantasauthor

https://twitter.com/KarinaKantas

https://www.youtube.com/channel/UC6c_j1bUSvYHj4Oq-Jw-YR-Q